THE GIRL WHO SAW LIONS

BERLIE DOHERTY

ANDERSEN PRESS

This edition published in 2018 by
Andersen Press Limited,
20 Vauxhall Bridge Road, London SW1V 2SA
www.andersenpress.co.uk
www.berliedoherty.com

First published in 2007 by Andersen Press Ltd as
Abela: The Girl Who Saw Lions

British Library Cataloguing in Publication Data available

ISBN 978 1 78344 646 9

Printed and bound in Great Britain by
Clays Ltd, St Ives Plc

1
ABELA

The priest arrived on a red motorbike. Dust rose like smoke around him as he roared into the village. Already the villagers were strolling towards the church, which was built like a barn on wooden supports. The sides were open, and swallows and children swooped and tumbled in and out. Abela had been one of the first to arrive, carrying her baby sister on her hip, the child's skinny arms looped round her neck. She was too big to be carried really, and Abela was too small to be carrying her. When she found her seat she lowered her sister on to the sandy ground and shook her shoulders to ease them. Nyota could walk now, but wouldn't. She sat gazing listlessly up at Abela, sometimes whimpering to herself, sometimes completely silent. The music and singing might distract her for a while, or might send her off to sleep. She was poorly, Abela knew that. There were many poorly babies in the village. Her grandmother, Bibi, told her there was no hope for any of them.

One of Abela's neighbours squeezed along the row to sit next to her. 'Where's your mama?' she asked. She had to shout over the noise of chattering and bird cries in the church.

'Mama's tired,' Abela said.

'She poorly too?' The neighbour clicked her tongue and shifted herself round in her creaking seat.

Abela turned her head away and watched the priest. She had nothing to say. Mama was sick. The baby was dying. Baba was dead. What was there to say?

The priest was unlocking the pannier of his motor-bike. He brought out a green carrier bag and took out his altar vestments, his long white robe, his gorgeous red embroidered chasuble and stole. He slipped them over his jeans and T-shirt and tucked his white collar into place. Then he walked into church carrying a tin of dried milk powder, which he placed on the altar table. He turned to face the congregation, and lifted his arms wide so his robes unfolded like wings around him. The chattering stopped. He began to sing, and immediately everyone joined in, fitting harmonies round his deep rich voice. The hymn was like a river flowing with currents of different colours. Abela always thought the sound she made when she was singing was yellow, golden-yellow like corn. Mama's was a pretty shivering blue. And Baba's – her father's – Baba's used to be brown. But Baba's voice would never be heard again.

'Please, please don't let Mama die too. Don't let Nyota die. Don't. Don't.'

If God listened to songs, he would surely hear hers, he would see the golden stream of her voice and listen to the words that floated inside it. And now the singing had stopped, and the priest was telling them that they must pray together for the dead and the dying and the sick.

2

Abela knew that the prayer was for just about everybody who wasn't in the church at that moment, and even for some people who were. Sickness stalked the village like a hyena, ears pricked, fangs dripping, sparing no family.

On the day Baba died, Mama had shaved her head to show she was in mourning for her husband. She sat outside their mud hut and all their belongings were brought out – their bedrolls, the cooking pots, the blankets and baskets. Her husband's younger brother moved into the hut, because he was nearly a man now, too old to be sharing a hut with his parents and his sisters.

On that terrible day of sadness Mama and Abela and the baby Nyota had sat in the baking sun waiting for someone to give them a home. With the help of her sisters, Mama had built the hut just before her marriage, slapping the wet red mud with her hands to shape it, piling the straw thatch onto the roof. When it leaked, she had smoothed mud over the cracks, smearing it to fill up the holes. Mama had dug the garden, their little shamba, and planted it with vegetables. She had spread out the beans to dry in the sun, she had pounded the maize to make flour, she had carried it to market in a banana leaf basket on her head. Even when Baba was ill she had done this, even when he was dying in the hospital. And when he died, they had been forced to give up their home and their shamba.

At last Mama's mother, the grandmother Bibi, had come to fetch them to her own house in the next village.

'One day soon,' Bibi had said, 'the hyena will come

for me, and this will be your home. And the field that goes with it,' she added, gazing out at the little strip of land that was their family's only wealth. 'Your brother won't want it, now he's in England-Europe.'

The priest used the key of his motorbike to prise open the lid of the dried milk tin, and brought out of it the discs of unleavened wafer bread. By the mystery of his prayers the bread would become the body of Christ. Abela knew that was so, even though it still looked like bread, and was so fine and light that it melted on her tongue and clung to the roof of her mouth.

'Lamb of God,' the priest said, 'Who takest away the sins of the world . . .'

The rainbow river of song poured through the church again, and the rich loud sound of it filled Abela with hope. God would hear it and make Mama well. Her golden voice shimmered all the way to heaven. Of course Mama wouldn't die.

The priest bowed and walked out of the church, with his powdered milk tin tucked under his arm. Outside the church he rolled up his gorgeous vestments in the carrier bag and returned them to the pannier. He swung his leg over the motorbike and turned the key. The bike roared into life, sputtering a cloud of smoke. Laughing children scattered away from him like dusty sparrows as he swerved round them and away to visit his next parish. Long ago, when he was a child, he had been one of the red-robed nomad children of the Maasai Plain, but that was before the Jesuits had given him an education and priesthood and called him John, after a saint, instead of by his tribal name. He had never been back to his tribe since his ordination.

We have a game, Mama and I, when we pound maize. When the corncobs have been drying in the sun for long enough, we shake off all the little yellow buds into a heap, and we pour them into a basket. They go *tchick, tchick*, as they trickle down. Then we grind the buds into flour. We pound it with the end of a long stick from a tree, which is just as tall as Mama. It takes so long that our legs ache and ache with standing and our arms are heavy with holding the branch and stamping it down again and again. We must do it for hours, every day when the corn is ripe, to make enough for our food, to make enough to sell. The sky is greasy and sweaty. Flies buzz round my face and walk on my skin, and because my hands are busy I can't brush them away. They crawl in my hair and I can't do anything about them. My head throbs and I'm thirsty and tired.

This is when the game starts. Just when I think I can't do any more, Mama shouts, 'One, Abela!' She raises her branch and then she lets go of it and she claps her hands before she catches it again. I do the same. It's hard to keep the pounding rhythm going. *Pound lift drop clap catch pound lift drop clap catch*. Mama sings while we're doing it. When we've got a nice smooth rhythm going she shouts, 'Two, Abela!' She lets go of her

5

branch and claps twice before she catches it again. *Pound lift drop clap-clap catch pound lift drop clap-clap*...My face is twisted with concentration and my hands are so sweaty that the branch slides through them. Mama is singing and my chest is tight with wanting to laugh. The rhythm flows, smooth as a dance, and then Mama shouts, 'Three, Abela!' But it's impossible. We bend over with laughter, it hiccups out of me like the little yellow buds of corn, and Mama's laughter peals out like pretty bells, blue and shivery and sweet. And when we look down, the flour is made.

But we don't play that game now. Mama doesn't stand with me while I'm pounding corn. She lies in the cool darkness of Bibi's hut, and she doesn't laugh any more.

I am not afraid of anything. I am not afraid of the mad mzee who comes down to the market sometimes. She is not like my grandmother mzee, Bibi. She is like a wounded animal. We don't have a proper stall in the market, under the shade of the thatch, because we are too poor. We spread a cotton kanga on the ground and sit on it, and Mama and I make little heaps of the things we have brought to sell; red beans sometimes, or yellow cobs of corn, or oranges that a neighbour has swapped with us. If we have been given green bananas we lay them out in a bunch, like the fingers of a hand. If we sell enough to buy some other food from someone else, we are happy.

But then the mad mzee comes hobbling round the

stalls with her panga tucked under her arm. This panga is a very sharp curved blade that is used for cutting down the corn. My father once told me that he had seen a man slice another man's head clean off his neck with a panga, because he had tried to steal his cow. And the mad mzee comes with her panga, muttering and grumbling and staring at people, and if she thinks you are a stranger or you are laughing at her, or she doesn't like your face that day, she waves her panga in the air and lurches towards you. I'm not afraid when she chooses me, because I can run, and she can only stamp her feet on the ground and stumble forward a few paces. I can run to the chilli-seller's stall and hide under it, and when the mad mzee finds me she bends down shrieking and wallering, and I see the blade like a silver tongue sipping the air for me. I can back away and shimmy under the next stall.

In the end she forgets me and chases another child or the white lady teacher Mrs Long, until somebody holds out a cigarette to her. This is what she wants. She tucks the cigarette behind her ear and shuffles away home, and the gossiping in the market starts again, and somebody puts on the tape of Mister Bing Crosby singing 'I'm dreaming of a white Christmas,' which we all love so much. No, I'm not afraid of the mad mzee.

And I'm not afraid of the lion. Simba. The lions live up in the purple mountains and they never come down to the village in the daytime. At night we sometimes hear the maize crinkling as they step through it, and we lie in the darkness with our breath as soft as moths, and my mama's hand creeps out to me and closes over mine. But Simba won't come into our hut, and we won't go out in the darkness of the night, so I'm not afraid of him.

I know how to kill a lion. My baba told me that when he was a boy he saw Maasai men killing a lion who attacked their cattle. It takes four men to kill a lion, Baba said. One dances in front, to lead him away to a safe place. One dances behind to grab his tail when he springs. And when it is safe, the other two men stab him with their spears, one each side. Then the Maasai men leap in the air and holler *lu-a-lu-a-lu-a-lu,* because their cattle are safe again. But nobody wants to kill Simba, Baba told me. He is beautiful, with his golden coat and his black mane. He is huge and proud and silent and strong, and he belongs to the lion world, not the man world. So I'm not afraid of the lion.

I am not afraid of the little monkeys who drop down on me from the trees and squeal and jabber down my ear and pull my hair with their tight little fists. They snatch food from my hands and gobble it up. I hate them sometimes, but I'm not afraid of them.

I have never been afraid of anything till now. Now I'm afraid that my mama is going to die.

2
ROSA

Far, far away from Africa, in a northern England city called Sheffield, it was beginning to snow. It came in such a short, sharp flurry that it was over before a lot of people knew it had started, but when they looked out of the window or left their offices and schools to catch the bus home, they found a white layer covering everything, softening all the sharp angles of the buildings, making the pavements slithery. It was not enough yet to make the city beautiful, or to bring the traffic to a halt. It just made everyone want to get home as quickly as they could.

The man who stood outside the Central Library every day selling copies of the *Big Issue* stamped his feet to try and keep himself warm. If he sold one more copy before it was dark, he decided, he would have earned himself a polystyrene mug of hot coffee from Zooby's in the Millennium Gardens over the road.

'Who'll buy my last copy?' he shouted. It was a little lie; he had ten more copies inside his coat, but it usually did the trick. A young woman came down the library steps, tucking her hair inside the collar of her coat, and took out her purse immediately. 'It's not very nice for you today, is it?' she said, taking the magazine from him. 'I don't want the change, thanks.' Her breath smoked away from her.

'Thanks a lot. Enjoy the snow,' the man said, and the woman hurried away into the warmth of Marks & Spencer's, where she bought a chocolate cake for her daughter's birthday tea, and then ran to catch the supertram home. She arrived outside the school at the same time as Rosa. She often did this. She wouldn't let Rosa walk through the park on her own on dark nights. If she wasn't there, Rosa had to walk the long way round, past the shopping centre and the junior school. The park was much quicker.

'What have you got there?' Rosa asked her.

'Nothing,' her mother said, and kissed her. 'Snow on your birthday! You spoilt brat!'

They walked deliberately across the grass as they crossed the park, making their footsteps the first in the snow. By the time they reached their house it was turning to sleet. 'We've had the best of it,' Rosa's mother said. 'It'll all be gone by tomorrow.'

'Ah,' said Rosa. 'I want it to snow all night! I wanted a day off school!'

They scurried down the echoey entry and through the back door, and Rosa immediately ran through the kitchen and the living room to see if any cards had arrived for her. There were two, from her uncles and aunts. 'To our darling Rosa,' one of them said. 'Have a wonderful wonderful birthday, Aunty Sarah and Uncle Robert.' There was a twenty-pound note inside.

'Ey up Duck,' the other one said. 'Have a cracking time. Lisa and Nigel' with a hand-drawn picture of a duck looking at an egg. There would be a book from them next time she saw them; there always was. She would devour it in one night, and then read it again and again.

Mum was standing in the kitchen, leafing through the *Big Issue* that she had bought in town. She opened it at a particular page and smoothed the spine down to keep it open there. She laid it flat on the table. Rosa glanced at it. It showed a picture of black children in a dusty compound. *A Desperate Situation*, the headline read. Twitchy jumped on top of the magazine and mewed plaintively to remind her it was food time.

'I got two cards,' Rosa said. 'And twenty pounds, Mum! *Twenty!*' She paused. 'And – ahem?'

'Nana and Grandpa will be bringing something,' Mum smiled. 'Help me clear up, love. They'll be here soon. I hope this snow doesn't hold them up.'

'What are we having?' Rosa asked.

'Guess.'

'Sausage surprise?'

'Got it in one.'

Rosa scrambled round the living room, hiding shoes under the settee and straightening up the heap of books by the coffee table. She pulled shut the yellow curtains and twitched them into shape, straightened the tartan blanket that covered up the threadbare patches that Twitchy had scratched into the armchair, then ran upstairs with her school bag.

11

'What shall I wear, what shall I wear?' she shouted.

'Something gorgeous!' her mother shouted back. 'Quick! They're here.'

Rosa was giggling with excitement. She opened her wardrobe door and clicked the clothes hangers along the rail one by one – blue dress, no, yellow skirt, no, brown skirt, no, green cords, no, blue jeans! She pulled out her new jeans with the flowery patch pockets and a red polo-necked sweater, wriggled out of her school uniform, and she was dressed and down the stairs before Nana and Grandpa came through the door. Grandpa lifted her off the ground and squeezed her against him like a cushion. His clothes and his beard were wet with sprinkles of snow.

'I can only just do that now!' he laughed. 'You're nearly a giant. Anyone would think you were thirteen years old.'

'I am! I am!' Rosa shouted, leaning back and pretending to batter him with her fists. 'Put me down, you monster!'

'Calm down,' Nana said. 'You're a young lady now, Rosa.' She opened up her carrier bag and brought out a present wrapped, as always, in Christmas paper. Nana never saw the point of buying special birthday paper, at any time of the year. Rosa looked at her mum excitedly. Was it, could it be, the present she had dreamed of? She tore open the paper, opened the box, and screamed with joy. It was. It was a pair of ice skates.

• • •

I love skating, more than anything else in the world. Mum and I are learning together. We go to the skating rink every Saturday morning, and we are in the same class. We're just about as good as each other. I can go backwards, I can spin, I can do cross-overs. I love the music, which makes me want to dance and sing, and the sounds of the skates *freeshing* on the ice. I love the excitement I feel when I try a new move, and try and try again because it's too hard at first, and then find out I can do it. Most of all, I love it because it's something my mum and I do together.

It was my idea. I was off school with a sore throat last winter and Mum let me sit by the fire with the tartan blanket round my shoulders, and watch daytime TV. It was the European Games, and I watched a girl of about fourteen doing figure skating. She looked so quick and graceful and neat, like a little bird, and I thought, I want to do that.

'What d'you think, Mum?' I asked her. 'I really, really want to learn to skate. D'you think I could?'

And Mum put her arms round me. 'If you really want to do it, you can,' she said. 'And do you know, Rosa, it's something I've always wanted to do, too. We could have lessons together, if you don't mind me falling over every five minutes and making a fool of myself.'

So we started having lessons, and to our surprise Mum turned out to be quite good at it, and so did I. We wouldn't miss our Saturday skating lesson for anything. Since we started ice-skating we've got into the habit of having to do particular things each time we go, a set of traditions like a sort of good luck charm. The first is that we always travel to Ice Sheffield on the supertram. The car won't do, because Mum doesn't believe in using a car when you can get there by public transport. The bus won't do, because the roads are so busy it might make us late. And the tram is perfect, because it glides so smoothly and quietly you could believe it was on skates and saying, 'Look at me! I can do it too!'

The best part of the journey is when we climb out of Sheffield centre, away from Pond's Forge and the big swimming pool with its see-through flume tunnels. Then the tram is soaring uphill, gliding us away from the city, and we're looking down on the shining canal and the smart hotel complex far below us. We're sky-skating. Mum and I smack our hands together and say, 'Yes! We're off!'

When we arrive at the Arena stop, I race Mum up the track to Ice Sheffield – I always beat her and have to wait at the door. Then she has to wait for me while I get my hire boots – I always sniff inside them to make sure they're not too sweaty from the last wearer, and then she has to lace them up for me because I can never get them quite tight enough; I'm too impatient. She has her own boots because her feet have stopped growing. She bought them on eBay, and they look about a hundred years old. Even the blades are a bit rusty, but she says that gives them character. She can lace them up in seconds while I'm hopping about. Then she takes off her purple skate guards and we hobble towards the ice. Just before we step on, she squeezes my hand.

'Don't...' she says.

'Break...' I say.

'Anything!' we both say, and then we're off, skating as fast as we can round the rink, and we lose each other because we're in a tide of people, all swaying and gliding, drifting, dancing. It's like the river swim at Pond's Forge; you just have to go with the current, leaning into the bends like a cyclist, round and round, swift and sure, a swarm of coloured fish. I know some of the people who come to coaching every Saturday, and we shout to each other as we pass. Mum's friend Pat swoops up to us and they swing along side by side, gossiping about growing beans or treating poorly cats or playing fiddle. Pat's son Jamie is my age. He skates faster than anyone, head down, knees bent, lapping us all. His little brother Toby does his best to keep up, and his cheeks glow like red roses with the effort. And then there's Paige, who skates like a ballet dancer, her arms willowy and her back straight and her head proud and high. Her hair is tied back in a pink band, and she wears a short pink skirt that flounces out when she turns; her skates have matching pink heels. I try to copy Paige, lifting my arms away from my sides like wings, but she looks like a swan floating across the water, and I look like a waddling duck, I just know it. I never even take my coat and hat and gloves off because it's too cold.

Our coaches call us into our groups and for the next

forty minutes we have to work hard, going backwards and forwards across the rink, swirling, making lemon shapes with our feet, scissoring, turning, weaving, going down on one knee and gliding up again. It's really difficult. I don't have time to look at anyone then, I just so much want to get it right. I'm only aware of one thing, and that's my ice shadow. She goes everywhere with me, turns with me, glides under my skates and comes round the other side. I know I shouldn't watch her because my eyes are supposed to be looking straight ahead, but it's like having a sister, a twin, my black self with me all the time.

When the coaching finishes the music comes on, and we're all grace and speed, all swans now, every one of us, floating free as air because we don't have to concentrate any more. We're all that little bit better than we were forty minutes ago. Paige floats towards me and away, backwards, and round, and away. I can hear Jamie stamping his skates on the ice, trying something new, scraping the pick, which is the little serrated bit at the tip of the blade, then he dashes past me, turns his head to grin at me, and tumbles over. He's up in the same movement, and his clothes sparkle with ice dust. Scrape, scrape, go Toby's blades; I can hear his sharp breaths, desperate to keep up. Then Mum's next to me, holding out her hand, and we glide round together. We both gasp and laugh out loud with the fun of it. Everything seems to fall away from us; all the skaters and the watchers and the coaches, it's just me and Mum, holding hands and looking at each other and laughing, ready to fly.

The thing about Mum is – I can't say this to her, I can't really say this to anybody, because it sounds a bit silly – but, well, I think she's my best friend. And that's why the skating, learning together and having fun together and holding hands and swinging each other round – that's why it's my favourite thing.

When the public come on we hobble off the ice, ducks again, and totter over to one of the tables at the rink side. This is another tradition. Mum has some coffee from her flask and I have a muesli bar, and we sit for a bit and watch the skaters. It's exciting watching the rush and swirl of all the coloured swans with their black shadows. There's a patch of sunlight coming through one of the high windows, and it makes a window shape on the ice. When people skate through it they turn briefly golden. Paige pauses in the centre of it and lifts her arms high, like a golden bird.

'We've passed to level nine today,' Mum told me one day, just before my birthday. 'We've got to decide what to do when we finish that. Figure skating or ice hockey.'

'Do we have to choose?' I asked her.

'If we still want coaching, we do.'

'Figure skating.'

'That's fine.' Mum poured herself another coffee. 'I'm thinking of doing ice hockey with Jamie.'

I stared at her. I couldn't believe it. This is what *we* do together; this is our special thing.

An Asian family stumbled past, one by one, just the other side of the barrier. They were all clinging onto the

17

bar with both hands, frowning with concentration. One of the boys dared to lift his hand away and disappeared completely, his feet slithering away in all directions.

I sniggered.

'That was us, twelve months ago,' Mum reminded me. 'We've done it, Rosa! We can skate! It just shows, if you really want to do something, if you really work at it, you can do it. Never forget that, will you?' She screwed the lid back on her flask. 'Back to the ice? Fifteen more minutes, then we'll have to catch the tram.'

I heard her, but I didn't move. I was watching Jamie, head down, charging round the rink as if all the bears in the woods were chasing him. Then down he went. Splat!

And not long after that, Mum told me about the adoption child.

We were on the supertram, on the way to Ice Sheffield for a public session. I shifted round in my seat to watch Sheffield slip away from us as we swooped up from Fitzalan Square, then I lifted my hand up for the hand slap and the 'Yes! We're off!' Mum didn't respond. She'd forgotten all about our tradition. I had noticed that she was behaving a bit oddly that Saturday morning. It was a bit like our first morning of skating; she seemed tense and nervous, locked inside herself. Looking back, I think she'd been a bit strange all week, making private phone calls from her room and saying she had meetings to go to in town as soon as she left me at school. She seemed to be happy and worried all at the same time;

and at last, that Saturday morning, she told me what was going on. She moved across from the seat facing me so she was sitting next to me, and said, 'Rosa, I've got something very special to ask you. How would you like to have a sister?'

I nearly burst with surprise and excitement. 'Mum! Really? Oh, cool! Are you going to have a baby?'

She shook her head, smiling. 'You're pleased, aren't you? But no, I'm not having a baby. I'm thinking of adopting a little girl.'

That was how she broke it to me.

'What do you think? What do you think, Rosa?'

What was I supposed to think? I said nothing, nothing at all. How could I say anything, there on the tram, or anywhere, how could I tell her how I felt? I didn't want an adopted sister. I didn't really want another child in our house at all. A baby was one thing, I could play with it and take it out in the pram. It might even look like me. But an adopted sister? What if I had said to her, 'I'm thinking of adopting a mother?' How would she have felt? Inside my head I was screaming. If I opened my mouth, all that would have come out would have been a scream.

She kept on talking to me but I wouldn't answer. She kept on and on, pouring words into my ears, words that I didn't understand and didn't want to hear and didn't have any answer to.

'I've always wanted a sister for you,' she said.

Scream, scream, scream inside my head, like the

19

whistle of a train as it dives into the tunnel.

'I never wanted you to be an only child, Rosa. We'd be a real family,' she said. 'What do you think, Rosa?'

I turned my face away from her and stared at my reflection in the window. Mum couldn't talk now, there were some kids opposite us talking and laughing noisily. She tried to hold my hand instead. I balled it up into a fist. She stroked the fist. She lifted my balled fist up and kissed it, and in my reflection I saw my eyes glisten with tears.

When we came out of the tram, the sun was blinding. Mum started chatting about whether we'd be able to do the lemon skating move without falling over today, where we have to bow our legs in and out.

'Now that we've passed level nine, you might be ready to have your own pair of skating boots, instead of using hired ones. I was wondering about getting some for your birthday. Shall we go and look at some today? You could try them on, and we can find out how much they're likely to cost.'

My own boots! I felt as if I had woken up from a bad dream. I watched her face, but that worried look had gone; she was smiling and chatting and promising me any colour boots I wanted provided I made sure my feet wouldn't grow one more centimetre from one birthday to the next. At last I trusted myself to look at her again. Maybe she wasn't going to mention this adoption business again. Maybe she'd forgotten all about it; and so would I. Maybe she'd realised that she had made a terrible mistake. And when we went into the shop at the ice rink and tried on the new boots, and found a pair, a pink pair with red heels, the most beautiful boots in the shop – then, at last, I allowed myself to smile at her again. In fact, I felt as if my cheeks might burst.

Mum screwed up her face when she saw the price.

'What d'you think?' I asked anxiously. I couldn't help clutching the boots to my chest and stroking them, as if they were a pet rabbit.

'I think Nana and Grandpa might chip in,' Mum smiled, and squeezed my hand. She asked the assistant if we could take the catalogue home with us, so I could look at the picture of them every day until I really owned them.

And that's today, my thirteenth birthday, the day of the glittering snow.

3
ABELA

During the night my grandmother Bibi woke me up, shaking my shoulder, hissing in my ear, 'Abela, Abela, get up now.'

It was pitch dark. My eyes were sticky with sleep. I rolled away from her and she shook me again, 'Abela, your mama's very sick.'

When there is no light there is no body, only a hissing voice and a hard hand gripping your shoulder. It brings fear; it brings such hopelessness, when there is no light anywhere. I fumbled across the floor to where my mother lay. She was so hot that I could feel her skin burning before I touched her. Hot, and wet, and her breath dry like wind-rattled leaves.

'Mama, what's wrong?' I whimpered.

'It's time to take her to the hospital,' Bibi said.

'Now?'

'Yes, yes, the sooner the better. I can't do anything more for her.'

I was still stupid with sleep, shaking with tiredness and fright. The hospital was in the town, more than a day's walk away for a fit man. I didn't understand what my grandmother wanted me to do.

'You must go with her, now,' she insisted. 'I'll stay

with Nyota.'

Numb, I wrapped my kanga round myself, and my grandmother put a blanket round my shoulders. Last year my mother and I had walked my father to the hospital, one each side of him, and he leaned on her the whole time. We had trudged and swayed and stopped, trudged and swayed and stopped. The sun had come and gone twice before we had arrived.

'How can I do it on my own?' I whispered. 'You must come too.'

'I can't,' my grandmother said. 'I must look after Nyota.' She had my sister in her arms, wrapped tightly in her kanga. I felt for her cold little baby hand, and knew then that I would never see my sister again.

'Bring her too,' I urged.

'And we'd walk as slow as elephants. No, take your mother, and go as quickly as you can. Maybe the doctors can save her. I can't.'

My mother groaned and sat up on the edge of her bed, and between us Bibi and I lifted her to her feet.

'Can you walk, Mama?' I whispered.

'Yes, I can walk.'

My grandmother put into our hands the poles we used for pounding the corn. 'These will help you,' she said, 'and you will be able to protect yourselves with them, too.'

I remembered once when I was very little, my baba gave me a long stick that would fight off lions. 'Look big and stern,' he used to say, 'and wave your stick at them. Shout your head off! Then see how Simba runs away.'

And he would laugh his honey laugh at the way I drew myself up to my full height and brandished my stick and roared at the pretend lions. It was a game, that day.

So we set out, with the blanket spread across Mama's shoulders and mine, even though my mother protested that she was hot. I could feel her skin raging like fire. The earth was cool under our feet. We could see that the sky was nearly white with stars that were as bright as fireflies. Nobody moved in the village, everybody slept, but as soon as we left the cluster of huts I knew that the beasts of the night were prowling, watching and waiting, stalking hungrily. Sometimes a sharp scream splintered the silence, and we knew that some creature had been taken. And the more I listened, the more I heard, creaking and scratching, padding and slithering; a quick yapping here, a flurry of wing beats there.

Mama leaned heavily on her stick, but after a bit she put her free arm across my shoulders, and I put my arm around her waist, and our moon shadow told us that we were one creature with two heads and six legs. We would have laughed about that, not long ago. We would have roared a two-headed roar that would have frightened a rhinoceros.

Sometimes Mama hummed a little tune, and sometimes I sang the lovely songs we learnt at school and at church. We were both glad when the light came at last, but the sky was a greasy grey and the air was clammy. It grew hotter and hotter, drumming with insects, and the road in front of us shivered in a haze of heat. Whenever we found shade

24

we sheltered in it. At midday, when the sun was a blazing yellow ball above our heads, we came to a place where little stalls were set up along the roadside. Some boys who were sitting with a pile of Coke bottles filled with water told us that the bus that went all the way from Dar es Salaam to Arusha should be passing by soon, and that maybe it would stop there to give the passengers a break. A little boy was standing next to a huge pile of smooth green coconuts. He hacked away at them by spearing them with a stick that he held on the ground with his toes. He had a knife between his teeth, and when he saw us he sliced the top off one of the coconuts and handed it to me. I gave it to my mother to drink the juice, and then the boy hacked out the wet flesh for me.

A woman who was cooking little cakes on a pot over a smoky wood fire told her son to give us some orange slices that he was preparing for the passengers.

'She going to hospital?' the boy asked, pointing his knife towards my mother. I nodded, squeezing the last juice from the orange, chewing the white pulp to a mush before I spat it out.

'You going on the bus?' his mother called.

'No money,' I said. 'We have to walk.'

'Tchk. She got no walking left in her,' the woman said.

'Just resting,' Mama said. She closed her eyes and curled up where she was sitting, and the woman clicked her tongue behind her teeth and came over to us, pulling her kanga off her shoulders and making a hood of it to shade Mama's face.

'You got a baba?' she asked me.

I said nothing. She blew out her cheeks and shook her head. '*Pole sana*,' she said. *I'm sorry.*

Suddenly the boys set up an excited shouting, waving their arms and skipping, as the cloud of noisy red dust that was a bus came bumping towards them. They ran to their piles of bottles and plates of quartered fruits, and balanced trays of hard-boiled eggs and maize cakes on their heads, jostling to be seen so people would buy from them. The people in the bus had been sitting for hours – some of them had been riding on it for over a day. They climbed out, stiff-legged, rubbing their eyes, stretching out their arms, bending their knees. The men went off to one side and the women went to the other, to relieve themselves in the bushes.

Among the passengers were two white women. One wandered away from the bus, and the other called after her, 'Don't go too far! There'll be snakes in the bushes!' then turned and came over to buy some of the little hot cakes and sliced mangoes and oranges that the people near us were selling. She had a pale blue cotton scarf wound round her hair and most of her face to protect her from the dust of the bus ride, but before she ate she pulled it away. Her hair shimmered golden-red around her shoulders, like a fire. I would like to touch that hair. She squatted on the ground by me, looking curiously at my mother, who was lying on the ground, not moving, clutching my hand in hers.

'Is she tired?' the woman asked in Swahili, my own language.

'No, she's sick,' the oranges boy told her. 'She's going to the hospital to die.'

I gave a loud sob then; it jerked out of me like a black fox jumping out of the grass, leaping out of its long hiding place. The woman looked at me, and her face was so soft with pity that I wanted to pick up my mother in my arms and run all the way back to Bibi's hut with her.

'Where is the hospital?' the woman asked. 'Will you go on the bus?'

'No money, Teacha,' I whispered shyly in my school English. My throat was clumped up so much with more hidden sobs that the words would hardly sound. She called her friend over and the two women talked to each other so quickly that I couldn't understand a word of it, but I watched them going over to the driver and talking earnestly to him, offering money. He shook his head, and then one of the women took out her purse and offered him more money, and then they were all smiling and nodding towards me. I knew they had bribed him to take us to the hospital.

When the driver was ready to move on, the women helped Mama onto the bus and sat her by the open window, with her kanga over her face to protect her from the dust. The village boys ran alongside the bus for a while, desperate to sell a few last things, and some of the passengers tossed their emptied Coke bottles back out to them. The boys dropped back as the bus picked up speed. They had missed school that morning, and they didn't care.

I sat on the floor of the bus, in the gangway, and the big boy who had given up his seat to my mother sat opposite me, laughing as we pitched from side to side on the rutted road. I laughed too, because I was so happy. The long, frightening walk was over and soon, soon now, we would be at the hospital.

The boy told me that during the night the bus had broken down for three hours, and that two men had tried to mend it. In the end the police had come and arrested the owner for having an unroadworthy bus, and taken him off to prison. I laughed again; I hugged myself with joy. If the bus hadn't broken down, we would never have seen it, and the white women wouldn't have paid for us to ride on it. The day was golden again. The oranges boy was wrong. My mother would get better.

4
ROSA

I was sure Mum had forgotten about the adoption child business. She didn't say another word about it, and neither did I. She must have decided it was a bad idea after all. And then, one afternoon a few days after my birthday, she wasn't at school to pick me up. Sophie Maxwell's mum said I was to go home with them instead, which meant that instead of walking through the park with Mum, I had to climb up into their huge people carrier and have two retrievers slobbering down the back of my neck. Our house is just across the park from school, too near to get the bus home, but Mum won't let me walk across the park on my own on dark nights.

'Your mam's got a visitor,' Sophie's mum said to me. She chews gum all the time because she's trying to stop smoking. *Slap slap slap* it went as she was talking. I could see her mouth in the driving mirror, *slap slap slap*, but I couldn't really hear what she was saying because of the dogs' heavy breathing.

'Has she got to come to our house?' Sophie asked. She doesn't like me much, and I don't like her, she just happens to live two doors away.

'Not likely,' her mother hissed. I heard that all right. She smiled sweetly at me in the driving mirror. When

29

she smiles her face pouches up, like when you go to the dentist and he puts a wad of cotton wool in each cheek. When we got to our house I clambered out thankfully, wiping dog dribble off my neck.

'You're welcome to come round to ours if your mam's still busy,' Sophie's mum called. Slap slap slap went her chewie.

'Not likely,' I muttered.

There was a strange woman in our kitchen, drinking tea. She had her hair in long grey plaits and she was wearing flowery trousers and the most beautiful red, green and blue shoes. If there's one thing I love even more than books, it's shoes. I'm going to design them one day, but that's my secret.

'So this is Rosa,' she said, and held out her hand, just touching my cheek. I backed away.

'Rosa, this is Miss West,' Mum said.

'Molly,' the lady said, smiling. 'I'm from the adoption society, Rosa.'

'Oh,' I said. I couldn't keep the disappointment out of my voice. So Mum hadn't forgotten at all. She had been holding it in her head, a private secret, all this time.

I made to run upstairs, but Mum gave me a look that said, 'Stay where you are,' and then a smile that said, 'Please, Rosa, don't let me down,' and then she really said, 'Rosa, get yourself a mug and have a drink of tea with us. And a chocolate biscuit.'

I did exactly as I was told. I was a sweet demure child. I ate my biscuit nicely and I answered the Molly lady's questions about school. I told her the dinners weren't bad and that my favourite lesson was Games, which made her laugh. She asked me who my best friend was and I said Sophie Maxwell because that was the only name that came into my head, and *that* was because although I was being sweet and demure on the outside, inside I was shaking. My whole stomach was shaking. My brain was shaking. All I could think was that if the adoption lady saw what a nice girl I was she would realise that Mum didn't need another one.

'Would you like to show me your room, Rosa?' the Molly lady said. I looked at Mum and she smiled at me, thanking me with her eyes for being so sweet and demure.

'It's a bit of a mess,' I confessed.

'Doesn't matter,' said Molly. 'So's mine.'

So we went up to my room, and she cooed over the pile of soft dolls and the poster of Doctor Who and the curtains with the border of teddy bears that Mum had made for me when I was born. I looked at it with a stranger's eyes and knew it was a child's room, not a teenager's. But I was comfortable there. I was safe.

'I'll show you what's best,' I said. 'You see that bookshelf? The gap in the middle? You have to throw one of the toys on from the bed, so it's sitting up, and you can't knock any books off. The clown does it best, because he's got long legs.'

I knew it was childish – a kid's game from stupid sleepover parties I used to have when I was about nine.

I felt like being childish, that's why. I grabbed two of the soft toys and demonstrated, and then Molly had a go and failed miserably, but she thought it was very funny. I showed her my skating boots, and because she looked so interested I said she could have the catalogue if she liked. She sat down on my bed and looked at all the boots in it, and said mine were definitely the nicest. I told her I liked her shoes, which made her laugh again. And just when I thought I'd been doing all the right things, she clasped her hands together and said, 'This is such a lovely room. How do you feel about having another bed in here, Rosa? Have you thought about what it will be like to share it with someone?'

There goes my stomach, jerking like a flapping bird. 'I don't know,' I said.

'You'd have to move all those soft toys, I would think.'

There was a long silence. I could hear Mum washing up the mugs and plates downstairs.

'Are you looking forward to it?'

'I don't know.'

'Tell me what you think about the idea.'

I said nothing.

'It will take a bit of getting used to,' she said. She flicked one of her plaits back over her shoulder. Thump, it went. 'And it won't be easy. Not for you, or for your mum, or for the child who comes to join your family.'

I looked towards the window. The teddy curtains are stupid, I thought. They belong to a little kid's room. I don't want them any more. I let the silence drag on, and so did Molly. I knew she was waiting for me to speak, but I couldn't think of anything to say.

At last she stood up. 'Talk to your mum about it. Tell her exactly how you feel. That's important. Sometimes it's hard to say what you really think. Thank you for showing me your room. It's lovely.'

I didn't look at her. I watched the beautiful shoes walking across my zigzag carpet and heard them padding down the stairs. I could hear her and Mum talking in the kitchen, and then the front door opening and closing, a car starting up, and still I didn't move.

Much later, when the sky was quite dark outside and I still hadn't put my light on, Mum called up to tell me that tea was ready. She was bright and cheerful; I would almost say she was happy.

'I bet you liked her shoes,' she said.

'I didn't notice her shoes.'

'Does she remind you of someone?' Mum asked. 'Oh, I know! She reminds me of that lady at the station, that day we lost each other.'

I didn't have the sense to think why Mum said that, not at the time. I just got caught up in the old story. 'The lady with the tea cosy on her head?' I giggled in spite of myself, because the day we lost each other was the worst day of our lives, and now the only way we can talk about it is by laughing about it.

It happened last year. We had been to London for the day, for the most wonderful day ever. We had been on the Eye and on a boat on the river, and we had seen the

Changing of the Guard. On the train on the way back Mum was talking to a Chinese lady who had a gorgeous baby and a squirmy little boy of about three. Mum's like that; she just talks to anyone and becomes best friends instantly. She doesn't realise how hard it is for me. I quite like listening to people, and watching them. As long as they don't talk to me, it's all right. As long as they don't expect an answer. So I was pretending not to notice the little boy pulling faces at me, just listening in while Mum and the lady were chatting as if they'd known each other all their lives.

When we arrived at Leicester, Mum helped the little boy off the train while the Chinese lady carried the baby over one arm and the folding pram over the other. I was watching from my seat. Mum actually stepped off our train onto the platform, and when she put the little boy down he ran away from her, right across the platform. I watched Mum running after him. He could have toppled off the other side of the platform if Mum hadn't caught him in time. By the time his mother had sorted out the pram and put her baby into it, Mum was carrying him back, but he was kicking and wriggling and she couldn't put him down.

Then the awful, terrible nightmare thing happened. My train started moving. I was on it. I was sitting in my seat. I was jumping up; I was running to the door. I was banging on the glass. And Mum was standing on the platform, holding that screeching, squirming child and staring at me, just staring, with her mouth wide open.

I thought I would never see Mum again.

I thought, How many million people are there in England? How will I ever find her?

I ran up and down the aisle from one door to the other. I just didn't know what to do. A lady with long grey hair and a stripy knitted hat like my great-nana's tea cosy, told me to sit in my seat and be very brave and she would find a guard and everything would be all right. She went down the train one way and came back and smiled at me.

'I'll try the other end,' she said. 'Stay there.'

After what seemed like hours she came back with a man in a green uniform, who winked at me and asked me if I liked chocolate. I tried to explain to him that he had to stop the train so I could run back to the last stop but he said I had to stay exactly where I was. I thought they were kidnapping me.

At last he came back to talk to me again. He winked at me again and then fished in his jacket and brought out a bar of chocolate, and said that everything was all right.

'Luckily for us, your mum went straight to the station master at Leicester, and he's phoned through to me. She'll catch the next train,' he told me. 'It will get to Sheffield an hour after this one does. So when we get there, all you have to do is wait in the station master's office there, and she'll come and find you.'

'Gosh, isn't that handy,' said the lady with the tea cosy. 'I'm getting off at Sheffield too, so I'll look after you till your mother arrives.'

And then she fell asleep, leaning her head against the

glass so her tea cosy tipped over one eye. I made the chocolate last two hours. I stared at every station sign to make sure it wasn't Sheffield. When we arrived, I woke the lady up and took her to the station master's office, and the station master, who was the tallest man I have ever seen, told us both to go and wait in the waiting room, which was stifling hot. The tea-cosy lady ran out of things to say to me, so she just sat beaming at me. But she was wearing flowery trousers and the most wonderful pink trainers with little white daisies printed on them; that's why she was like the Molly woman.

I stared at the clock in the waiting room, and the fingers jerked and stopped, jerked and stopped, as if they hated the idea of ever moving again. And when at last the door opened and Mum walked in, we hugged each other so hard that it hurt, it really hurt. I felt as if I would never let her go. That's the only time, ever, that I've been anywhere without my mum.

'Gosh,' said the tea-cosy lady. 'Isn't it wonderful!' And she just melted away, waved through the window at us, and vanished.

'She was a bit like Molly,' I giggled. 'But I liked Molly's shoes much better.'

'Ah, so you did notice them,' Mum smiled. 'You see, Rosa. About us adopting a child. Imagine what it must be like not to have a mother or a father. To be completely alone in the world. Don't you think it would be lovely to be able to give a home to someone like that?'

• • •

It didn't help, being told that. I've lost my dad, too. I don't want a sister or a brother. I never have wanted one. I like it that it's just me and Mum. And if it really happens, this adoption thing, it'll never be just us again. I'll have lost my mum.

5
ABELA

Mama slept most of the way to the hospital, her hands fluttering and clasping each other in her lap as if they were talking to one another. When we arrived, I woke her up and helped her down the aisle and off the bus. She could hardly stand up, but she clasped the hands of the white woman with the red-gold hair, and thanked her. Then she thanked everyone in her tiny weak voice, nodding and smiling, and so did I. I was so happy that morning.

The white woman with the lion-coloured hair followed me off the bus.

'Wait, child,' she said.

I turned round to her. She held out some money to me, and when I shook my head, she pressed it into my hand.

'It's not much, I'm afraid, but you'll need this to buy medicine for your mother. Take it.'

I knew she was right. 'Thank you, Teacha,' I said in English, just as we're taught to do in school.

She smiled. 'I'm not a teacher. Just a tourist, enjoying your beautiful country.'

I think that's what she said. I know the word 'tourist' means *mzungu*. I don't know what a tourist does though.

I turned away, and she called me back again. 'Here,

you'll need food,' she said. She gave me a handful of sweet doughnuts wrapped in a banana leaf, and some bananas, the ones she had bought at the stop where she met us. 'Look after yourself, too. Your mother needs you.' The bus driver tooted his horn, revving up the engine, and she hurried back and climbed on, wrapping the blue scarf round her hair and face again. I strained my eyes, but I couldn't see her as the bus swung round in its cloud of red dust. I saw the boy who had given Mama his seat, grinning at me, and I laughed and waved.

'All right now,' I said to Mama.

She smiled weakly, and sighed. 'Yes, all right now.'

The hospital was a long, low concrete building, painted white. Crowds of people were milling round it, sick people and their relatives and friends. Some were lying on the ground, some squatting and staring mutely in front of them as if they were looking into their own future and seeing nothing. Some were gossiping as if it was the market, some were sitting apart and alone, waiting, waiting. A sick man arrived propped on a black bicycle; his arms draped over the shoulders of his mother and father who were supporting him on either side. Behind him trailed his wife and children, carrying clay cooking pots and coloured sheets, bedrolls, little bags of food. Someone shouted, 'The water's on!' and there was a rush of women from inside the hospital, carrying the soiled and bloodstained sheets that they

39

had pulled from the beds of their sick relatives. They clustered round the taps, scrubbing the sheets with their fists, jostling each other to get it done before the cold water was turned off again.

Abela and her mother threaded their way into the building. The smell of sweat and sickness was overwhelming. At least it was cooler inside than outside; the electric fans had been switched on at the same time as the water. Rows of iron-railed beds lined the walls, and in them lay the dying, and round them clustered their relatives, feeding them, washing them, stroking them, arguing over their heads. A few had grey, greasy nets slung above the bed, splodged with dead mosquitoes. Every now and then an ululating cry went up, 'Lu-lu-lu-lu-lu-lu-lu.' It was the cry of grief.

Those who had chosen to go home to die were carried out in the arms of their relatives. They were as thin and weak as baby birds. The weary nurses walked from bed to bed, doing what they could. They wore immaculate starched headdresses like white crowns on their heads. One of them sang, in a deep, croaky voice, as she trudged around the ward. It was as if it was only the singing that was keeping her going.

And into this stinking hellhole Abela and her mother walked. If she thought her mother had the strength, Abela would have turned round and taken her home again, walked through the sticky days and the lonely nights with her; anything rather than leave her here. As it was, she knew that all her mother wanted was to lie down and sleep. She watched a nurse throwing a stained sheet off an empty bed, and steered her mother towards it. Her mother sank down gratefully onto the filthy mattress and smiled up at Abela.

'Good girl,' she whispered, like a sigh of wind. 'You go home now.'

'No,' said Abela firmly. 'I'm staying with you, Mama. I'm going to make you better.'

Her mother's eyes glistened. She turned her head away and fell asleep.

Abela sat on the edge of the bed and watched the bewildering bustle of the ward. So many people. So much noise. She saw a boy of her own age come weaving in and out of the lines of beds with a live hen clutched in his hands. He was trying to catch the attention of one of the white-crowned nurses, but she seemed to ignore him. The hen clucked and squawked in shrill indignation, pecking the boy's fingers. At last the nurse turned round. Her eyes were nearly shut with weariness. The boy thrust the hen towards her.

'Please can I buy medicine for my father?' he asked.

The nurse shook her head. 'You'd do better to take your kuku outside and cook it. Make a nice tasty stew for your baba instead.'

'Please,' the boy begged. 'Mama said we haven't any money for medicine.'

'I said no.' The nurse walked on past him. 'Take your hen away.'

Abela remembered the money that the woman from

the bus had given her. She ran after the nurse and tugged her arm. 'I've got money,' she said. 'Some medicine for my mama and some for his baba. Real money.'

She held out her hand. The coins were hot and wet in her palm, she'd been clutching them so tightly.

The nurse clicked her tongue impatiently. 'Money or hens, mangoes or bicycles, they're no use, child. Nothing is, any more. We haven't got any medicines left. We ran out of them two weeks ago.'

Abela stared at her, unbelieving. They had come all this way for help. Surely there was something her mother could be given to ease her? The medicine man in the village would have found something for her, a weed or a herb, a coloured potato, the juice of crushed insects, anything rather than send her away with nothing.

'Can I pay for a doctor to see her?'

'No doctors here,' the nurse said. 'They've all moved on, or died. Your money is useless, little one, wherever you got it from. You can't even eat it. The only thing you can buy here is coffins.' She squatted down, moved at last by pity for the desperate child. 'Go home. Take your mama home. That's best. There's nothing we can do for her.'

Abela turned away from her, more upset by the hopelessness in the nurse's eyes than she had been by her earlier harshness. She hoicked up a corner of her kanga to make a pocket, tied the coins into it and tucked it into her waist. She went back to her mother and sat by her, bleak and cold now, the joy of the morning all gone.

42

The woman who was washing her daughter in the next bed called over to her, 'Medicine truck will be coming tomorrow, that's what I've heard. Why don't you get your mother some water? They'll be turning it off soon, and there'll be no more today.' She handed Abela a Coca-Cola bottle without a cap.

Abela was glad to have something to do. She ran out to the tap in the yard and waited in the queue, and at last her turn came. The bottle was only half full when the trickle of water stopped. She saw the boy who had been talking to the nurse standing listlessly, still clutching the hen. The bird squirmed in his hand, tapping his fingers with its beak.

'The medicine truck is coming tomorrow,' she told him. 'It'll be all right then.'

He looked at her blankly.

When her mother woke up, Abela tried to feed her with bits of broken biscuit and crushed banana, but she hardly ate anything.

'You,' she gestured to Abela. 'You have it.'

'No, Mama. You eat it.'

'You need it to keep strong,' her mother said. She closed her eyes and turned her face away. 'Be strong, my Abela.'

When night fell, sudden and full, some of the people outside the hospital lit their little paraffin lamps and built fires out of sticks, balanced their cooking pots on three stones over the flames, and heated up chicken bones and beans or whatever bits of food they had brought with

43

them. Some rolled themselves up by their fires to sleep. Others swarmed into the ward and stretched out on the floor between the beds. Abela climbed into bed with her mother, wrapped her arms round her, and slept deeply from utter weariness.

6
ROSA

Outside, the wind was hurling itself against the house as if it was a person, alive and angry. I could hear its voice. I could see how its breath shuddered the trees and tore the last dead leaves away. It was winter now, all right.

I was at my nana's house, sitting on the windowsill in the room that's my own bedroom there when Mum's away. This time Mum had been on a special one-day course about fostering and adoption, and because it was in London she spent the night with a friend. She was due back at tea time. I watched her arriving, but I didn't go down to her. After a bit I heard her going out again.

My nana is just the best person in the world, next to Mum. She has to be two grandmothers in one, as I don't know my dad's parents. She's always busy. She does voluntary work for a charity called Shelter, who care for the homeless, she has an allotment where she grows just about every misshapen vegetable you can think of, and she runs some kind of online self-help service. She's always going to meetings and phoning people up and bashing things out on her laptop, but when Mum and I go round she just puts all that business away somewhere else and makes a fuss of us. She would never, ever, let us come to the house without offering us a meal.

She called me downstairs to the kitchen soon after Mum went out.

'Come and give me a hand, Rosa.'

I went down the stairs slowly. I was feeling hurt and resentful. 'Where's Mum gone?' I asked.

'I just wanted a bit of shopping, so she's nipped up the road for it,' Nana said. She put her head to one side. 'You didn't think she'd gone home without you, did you?'

'I don't know,' I said. 'How would I know what she's doing?'

'Don't snap, crocodile,' Mum would have said, but Nana just smiled.

'Well, she could have taken you with her, but I pleaded with her to let you stay behind because I needed an expert cook around. Fancy making a lemon cake with me? I've got some eggs that need using up.'

She got out all the ingredients, and while she was melting butter and sugar in a pan I grated the lemon without shredding my fingernails. I tipped it into the melted butter, and Nana said, 'What do you think of this idea of your mother's? Are you pleased?'

I looked up at her. Nana is the only person that I can say just anything to, anything in the world. But my throat was clogged as if it was full of flour. My eyes were smarting. I tried to wipe them, pressing them with the back of my wrist.

'You crying, Rosa?'

'It's just the lemon juice.' But I was crying. I was crying inside.

'I'll tell you what I think,' said Nana. 'I think you're the most beautiful child I know, and so does Grandpa, and so does your mum. Oh yes she does. And I don't think any child in the world is more loved than you are.'

Now my eyes were bubbling, but I didn't let the tears run. I looked at Nana instead and smiled.

'Look at you, sunshine and showers, that's my Rosa.' She lifted the pan onto the table. 'Oh Lord, we haven't beaten the eggs yet. Do you want to do one? Watch me.'

She took one of the eggs out of its box and tapped it smartly on the edge of a bowl, then dropped in the golden yolk in its slimy mucus. I did the same, holding my breath in case the shell went in too. Two yolks, side by side. I stared down at them.

'Your mum's got so much love to give,' said Nana. 'She's always thinking about people who have nothing – no money, no home, no one to love them. She's been brought up to care about others, and so have you. Always looking for ways to help them. Here, Rosa.' She handed me the egg whisk. 'Mix 'em up.'

I turned the handle. The two golden yolks bobbed about like fish in a pond.

'Faster now!' Nana said.

The yolks broke and poured golden lights into each other. I whisked them faster and faster, and they both disappeared into a creamy yellow sea. I tipped it all into the mix, and Nana stirred in the flour and then poured the whole lot into the cake tin.

'What I love about cake,' she said, 'is that you put all

47

these separate ingredients in and when they're cooked, you can't taste any of them, just cake. If the mix is right. Just delicious cake.' She put the tin in the oven and eased it shut with her knee. 'She's got a lot of love to spare, your mum. She's got to put it somewhere.'

Grandpa put his head round the kitchen door and said if the chief chef was free he could do with someone to play a duet with, as he'd only got two hands. He teaches me to play the piano, a bit at a time, whenever I go round there. He says I'll soon be able to play better than he does, though he says that's not much to boast about. When we're playing duets I concentrate so hard that I forget to breathe sometimes. Grandpa's glasses slide to the end of his nose and I can tell he's twitching his face to try to keep them on, because the rule is, whatever happens, even if you lose your place in the music, to KEEP ON PLAYING. 'Don't stop! Don't stop!' Grandpa shouts, when I've got myself into such a mess that every note is wrong. His fingers gallop across the keys and I'm rolling about on the piano stool trying to remember to breathe, with laughter tears running down my cheeks. But we do it, we get to the end together, and bang down the last chord in triumph.

Silence. But the ghost of the music hums and throbs round the furniture all on its own.

And that day, in that buzzing silence, I heard Nana say, 'I don't think Rosa's very happy about this business, you know.'

I wondered whether she was talking to Grandpa, but

if she was, he didn't hear her. He was twitching through the pages of the duet book looking for something else to play. Maybe Mum had come back in without us hearing her, but she wasn't answering either. I was beginning to think I'd imagined it, when Nana said, 'I think you need to talk to her properly.'

Then Mum. 'I will, I just need to be absolutely sure about it myself. It's a big thing.'

'Well, don't leave it too long. She needs to be sure, too. I'll tell you something – your dad thinks you must be out of your mind, doing this to her.'

Crash! went Grandpa's hands on the keys. '"Jolly Miller",' he shouted. 'We haven't done this one for ages. Come on! Keep up!'

Mum's hobby is aromatherapy massage. It's just the most wonderful experience, the way her hands press firmly and steadily over your back or whatever part of you hurts, and she strokes the lovely bright-smelling oils into your skin. I feel as if I've been sleeping in a field of flowers when she does it to me. And I love the names of the oils – citronella, with its lemony smell that helps you to sleep; cassia, as warm and spicy as Christmas pudding; ylang ylang, which means flower of flowers. And Mum's favourite is vetiver, which means the oil of tranquillity. Mum loves to try and make people feel better. She treats people who are in pain with back problems or headaches or who just can't relax. Nana always seems to have backache, and when we come Mum always gives her a session, stretching her neck and pressing her spine, soothing her perhaps with a little rosemary and lavender in sweet almond oil. She'll lecture her for curling up on the settee when she's reading.

'You've got terrible posture, Mum,' she says to her. 'No wonder you're always in pain.'

I could hear them in the bedroom, while I was arranging salad on the plates; Nana mumbling contentedly under Mum's magic stroking, and then I heard Nana say, 'I won't go on about it, but are you sure you're doing the right thing, Jen? I'd hate Rosa to feel she was being rejected.'

I didn't hear Mum's reply, but Nana was absolutely right. That was just how I did feel. Rejected.

7
ABELA

I stayed with Mama in that hospital all that week, but no medicine truck came, no doctors. Mama grew so weak that she couldn't do anything for herself. There were no sheets for her bed. I used some of my money to buy two cotton kangas from the family of a woman who had died, and used them in turn. Every day when the water came on, I would roll Mama over and pull away the one she was lying on, and spread the other one out as carefully as I could, with no lumps and creases to hurt her. Then I followed the other women and girls to the taps and scrubbed the soiled kanga as best as I could, but they never came clean again. I spread it out in the sun to dry, ready for the next day. Then I took some water in the Coke bottle and washed my mother down with it, and last of all, gave her some to drink.

Sometimes people gave me bits of food from their pots. Somebody gave me a coconut and pierced it for me, and I trickled the sweet milk into Mama's mouth. I could see that she loved it. I sat on somebody's grating stool and shredded the coconut meat, and the owner of the stool boiled it with her sweet potatoes and filled my coconut shell with it for our meal. They were like a village, those people outside the hospital, and the boy with the hen and

51

all the other children who were on their own wandered from group to group, grateful for any scraps that people gave them. An old man with a beard like a cloud of froth called me over every day to give me a handful of his cooked maize. I got to know their names, and it was like another life, and I would be living there for ever.

But after the first week, Mama stopped eating or drinking. She could only stare at me, and her eyes were so fevered and burning that I wanted to close them for her so I couldn't see her pain. The only thing she said to me after that first week was this:

'Be strong. Be a strong girl, my Abela.'

I couldn't sleep in her bed any longer. She burned like a fire. I slept on the floor at the side of it, and when I didn't sleep, I listened to the sighing and groaning, the weeping round the ward, and I was no longer afraid of any of the noises. They were only the sounds of sick people. 'One day, I'll learn how to make people better,' I said out loud. 'And I'll come back and make you all well again.'

I went out next day as usual when the water came on. The pattern of the day was like a song, and I knew the words off by heart. Change kanga, wash it, fill bottle, wash Mama, find food. But when I came back, the singing nurse was standing by Mama's bed. She was still singing, her own low, deep song like a flowing river, but the white wings of her headdress hid her face from me. When she heard me coming she turned towards me and her eyes told me everything. I was filled with a cold, terrible, terrified dread. And my song came from me, from deep inside, and there is no stopping it when the grief is on us; it's the sound we make when someone has given up their soul at last; the song of death.

For three days Abela lay under her mother's bed, refusing to move. The nurses gave up trying to make her go away; they were too busy. After a time they stopped noticing her. When at last she crawled out she saw that there was a stranger in Mama's bed now, someone who looked like Mama but wasn't her, someone with arms like sticks and eyes as bright as burning coals. Abela went outside slowly, shielding her eyes against the blinding light of the sun. This hospital that had been like a whole world to her for weeks on end was an alien place now. She didn't belong here any more. She had to go home. The water was running again, and she filled up her plastic bottle at the tap, knowing dimly that she would need it on her journey. She must walk towards the morning sun, she knew that too. She knew nothing else. She was numb and cold and deeply afraid. She set off along the road towards the blinding orange sun, then stood aside as a van trundled towards her. There was a shout behind her and she saw people running to meet the van, yelling, cheering, banging on the sides, holding out their hands.

'Wait, wait, please wait!' Abela saw a boy break away from the crowd round the van and come running towards her, waving his arms in the air. It was the chicken boy. She waited, staring blankly at his excitement.

'Come back!' he shouted, as he drew near her. 'It's the medicine van! The medicines have come!'

Medicine. She frowned, searching deep inside herself to find the meaning of the word, or the significance of the boy's excitement. He had reached her now, and he stood in front of her, gasping for breath, his hand stretched out towards her.

'Medicine,' he said again. 'You can buy medicine to make your mother better.'

Tears blocked her eyes, just standing on the rim, refusing to flow. The boy was no more than a dark blur now, the shouts of the people clustered round the van made no sense to her. They were not like people noises. They were sounds from the air and the earth; the wind and the rain and the trees. The boy's voice came to her again out of the mysterious swirl of sound, and the words he made dropped like stones at her feet. She frowned at the dusty soil.

'Money,' the boy said again. 'For my father. To make him better.'

Now she understood him. She lifted up the corner of her kanga and untied the knot she had made in it, very slowly, because her fingers were stiff and numb and seemed not to belong to her at all, and then she handed the boy the coins that the white woman had given her. Without a word the boy turned and ran away, back to the van, back to the voices of the earth, the voices of hope.

Abela stumbled on towards the sun. When it was directly over her head she found some shade and slept a little, and then walked on with the sun behind her. Sometimes people came out of the trees towards her, slipping past her and out of her life as silently as they had come; ghost people, the people of dreams, the silent ones. She thought she saw her mother holding out her arms and smiling to her, but when she ran to her it was the light of the low sun on the blue smoke from someone's fire. An old man was roasting corn, and held out a cob for her to take. She ate it greedily. His wife hobbled out of her hut and *tcjkked* in her cheek at the sight of Abela's swollen feet.

'Stay the night here,' she told her. 'It's dangerous to walk now. You can curl up by the fire, nothing will harm you.'

But Abela couldn't stay. She didn't want anyone looking at her, or touching her, or asking her questions that she was afraid to answer. While the old woman was sprinkling the flames of her little fire with drops of water, Abela slipped away from her.

The sun had gone completely now. Fireflies danced like bright blue flames, then darted away. The sky was brilliant with clusters of stars, and the moon blazed in its own white brightness. Abela walked quickly, listening in her head to her mother's pretty blue voice. Then suddenly the song stopped, and Abela froze. There came another sound, and Abela knew that it was not inside her head but was part of the living darkness around her. The sound was stealthy and smooth, feet padding on crinkled stalks, strong bodies pushing canes aside, swift now, and purposeful.

That was the night she saw the lions.

I knew what they were before I even saw them. I didn't know whether to run away or to stay still. I wanted to lie down and wait. My bones were so tired that I just wanted to sink down onto the ground and sleep. I no longer knew where I was walking to or from, or why. I just wanted to sleep. Then the moon glided out from behind a tree and I saw the lions, and they saw me. There was one male and two lionesses. They were as still as statues, and they looked as if they were made of gold. Their eyes gleamed in the moonlight. *Please, please, holy God who comes with the priest to our church, don't let them kill me. Please. You have already taken my mother and my father. Please let me live.* These were the words that were beating in my head like drums, so fast that they weren't words at all, so loud that they drowned my heartbeats and the tremble of my breath. And my mother's voice was singing through them, *Be strong, my Abela, be strong.* I felt her standing by my side. I felt my father standing behind me, with his hands on my shoulders. I was as still as they were, as silent, as watchful.

And at last the lions left me. They turned their heads and padded away, shimmering black and gold through the trees.

I was alone again. The huge silence of the night

wrapped itself around me. The massive stars gleamed down on me like eyes. *Thank you*, I whispered. I let my voice trail out of me, and there was no answering roar. I was quite safe. I began to walk again, quickly this time, and then when I reached the road I began to run. I had thought I wanted to die, but when I saw the lions, I knew I wanted to live.

By the end of the next day Abela was back in her grandmother's house. There was no need to tell Bibi what had happened. The old woman held out her arms to her and rocked her, and they wept together. She gave her some soup and then wrapped her up in her arms again and they slept together on the mattress. It was a whole day before Abela woke up again. She lay listening to the village sounds outside the hut: children laughing, hens clucking, the steady chip, chip, chip of someone chopping wood. Everything was right again. Nothing was right.

She ran outside. Her grandmother was bent double, chipping a log to make kindling for the cooking fire. She was too weak to swing the axe like Mama used to do. Chip, chip, chip went the axe, sending little white splinters like sparks into the air. When she saw Abela she straightened up slowly, easing her back with one bony hand, wiping away the sweat from her brow with the other.

'Bibi, where is she?' Abela asked, though, of course, she knew. Her sister's little sleeping mat had gone. They had lost Nyota, their little star.

• • •

I don't know why God did this to me. He has taken nearly everything that belongs to me, and I am so afraid because I don't know where it will stop. Perhaps my grandmother will be the next, but she says no, she is too old to die of this sickness, she will die of something else.

'And me?' I hardly dared ask such a question. Fright was fluttering in my throat like a butterfly.

Grandmother Bibi shook her head. 'Your mama and baba were not ill when you were born, they were healthy and strong. But by the time they were waiting for Nyota to be born, they were already very sick themselves. So the baby had no chance.'

'No chance?'

'No. That baby had no chance to live.'

I stared into the pile of chippings that my grandmother had made. I have heard of a baby who was born with no sight. I have even heard of a baby born with no arms. But I have never heard of a baby born with no chance. And this was a new thing for me to think about; to live or to die, to be sick or to be healthy, was it all a matter of chance? Could this be true?

8
ROSA

OK. I wasn't quite a hundred per cent truthful about the skating. It wasn't easy at all. The first day we went to the ice rink, when I was so excited that I could hardly breathe, Mum made me sit for a bit watching the other skaters. They drifted like colourful butterflies across the ice, just flitting here and there, no effort at all. They looked wonderful. I imagined myself with them, gliding and spinning, weaving forwards and backwards with my arms outstretched like graceful wings, just like them. I picked out a girl in a pink skirt with matching boots, a *Swan Lake* girl, and I thought, That's me!

'Ready?' Mum asked me at last.

'READY!' I giggled. I couldn't wait.

So we hobbled across the rubber floor and stepped out onto the ice, and immediately my legs shot away from me and I thumped down on my bottom. The ice was hard and cold, and it really hurt. What was worse, I couldn't get up again. My skates slid away from me whenever I tried. I had to scrabble over onto my hands and knees and Mum hoisted me up into a standing position; then my feet splayed away from me again and I clung onto her for dear life. She was laughing, but I was close to crying with surprise and shock and hurt.

Mum planted my hands on the rail that ran round the rink, and that's how I spent the next half hour, totally glued to it, daring myself to move my feet more than an inch at a time. Even then, every now and again my feet betrayed me and shot away in any direction, and down I went. I banged my bottom, my knees, my chin.

Mum seemed to get the hang of it straight away, but she stayed near me, coaxing me round. When I'd managed to crawl right back to the starting point again I'd had enough. My hands were aching from clinging onto the rail, my jaw ached from gritting my teeth, my head ached from concentrating so hard. I stumbled out onto the mat at last. Mum went round the rink on her own then, very slowly, her hand just dithering above the rail in case she lost her balance and had to grab for it, but she did it, smiling with triumph, and then she came tottering over to where I was sitting. She brought out her flask of coffee and the muesli bar that I'd chosen so joyfully and hopefully on my way to Ice Sheffield that morning.

I shook my head when she pushed the muesli bar towards me. My throat was clenched tight, and my eyes were stinging with hot tears. *I'm not coming again. Never, never, never.*

'What hurts most, your pride or your bottom?' Mum asked.

I giggled in spite of myself, in spite of the tears that were washing freely down my cheeks.

'That's my brave Rosa. Sunshine and showers,' Mum said.

I turned away. Through my tears I watched the blurred pink *Swan Lake* girl. I wondered if she had ever, ever in her life, fallen over on the ice.

Mum followed my gaze. 'One day, you'll skate like that,' she told me. 'If you want to, that is. But you have to want to, very, very much.'

I swallowed hard, and bit the muesli bar. It was sweet and comforting.

Mum screwed the lid back on the coffee flask. 'We could go straight home,' she said, 'Or we could go round just once more. I could hold one of your hands, and you could hold the bar with the other, and I bet you'll be able to let go of the bar before we get back to the start again.'

And that's exactly what we did. It was wonderful!

It was about a month after her first visit before Molly came again. Mum had been to a couple of meetings with her in between and told me what happened there. I pretended to listen, but I was humming quietly in the back of my mind while she spoke, drowning out her words with the words of a song we'd been learning for the Christmas concert at school. In the concert, I sang a solo verse, and I was shaking so much that Ellen next to me had to hold the music. I daydreamed about that, and about the fact that Nana said it had made her cry to hear me singing, and that took me to the end of Mum's explanations and left me smiling sweetly and blankly at her when she finished.

A few days after the start of the new term, Mum asked

me if I'd like to help her to make some apricot slices. 'Why?' I asked suspiciously. They were my speciality. I only made them for special visitors.

'Molly's coming round after school,' she said. 'She wants to talk to you again.'

Aha. 'I've got homework to do,' I said. 'I can't waste my time cooking. Have you soaked the apricots?'

'Of course.' Mum lifted the lid of the pan, and the sweet sharp smell rose up to greet me. I nearly gave in.

'You need to boil off a bit of that liquid,' I said. Then I swung away and made as much noise as I could going upstairs. I threw my school bag on my bed and the French dictionary slid out onto the floor with a satisfying thud.

'And I'm not tidying up my bedroom,' I shouted. 'It's good enough as it is.'

I took out my favourite shoes, the red sequin ones that Aunty Lisa had given me for Christmas, and which I'm supposed to save for parties. I never go to parties, not since my best friend Zeena left, abandoning me to the likes of Sophie Maxwell and her party Mafia. No one who Sophie didn't like got invited to any parties. But who cares? I still had the shoes, and they are just about the most beautiful shoes I have ever seen. I turned off my bedroom light so only the light from the landing came into my room, making the shoes sparkle and glow like points of fire. I clipped my heels together like Dorothy in *The Wizard of Oz*, but nothing happened, nothing to whisk me away till Molly's visit was over.

Nothing ever does happen, in real life. If something awful is going on in your life you just have to stay put and get on with it.

I could smell the juicy apricots simmering in the pan downstairs; I could hear Mum thudding the rolling pin onto the pastry. She really hates making pastry, and the pastry knows it. She usually buys frozen or asks me to do it, saying I've got lovely cool hands and hers are too hot and sweaty for pastry making. I hoped she would remember the cinnamon.

The threatened visit lurked at the back of my brain all day at school, and it happened just as Mum said it would; there was no escape. When I arrived home, tipped out of the Maxwell smelly dog-transporter, Molly was there in her disappointingly rather scuffed-looking gorgeous shoes, sipping tea and chewing tough apricot slices. Mum had forgotten the cinnamon, and when I glared at her she took the plate to the pantry and shook a drum of mixed spice powder over the slices. It made us all cough.

I wore my sequin shoes again, and they were much admired by Molly. She told me about a pair of patent leather shoes she had been given when she was my age, and how she would shine them with the sleeve of her cardigan till she could see her face in them. She asked me about skating, and whether I'd learned any new moves since she last saw me. Fool that I was, and a born show-off, I demonstrated the knee bend, sliding about in my sparklers across the kitchen floor, which made her laugh and cough again.

And then, just when she had crossed the enemy line and had become a friend, she said, 'If we do find a sister for you, would you like to teach her to skate?'

I stopped immediately, in mid-flight, one knee bent and the other leg stretched behind me, perfectly balanced and frozen solid now as if the kitchen was full of ice, as if I was carved out of ice, as if she and Mum were two ice maidens.

From somewhere deep inside the heart of a glacier, Molly said, 'Rosa, you're not really happy about the idea of adopting, are you?'

I was too stiff and cold with ice to say anything.

'We need to have a proper talk about this. I'm trying to imagine how I would have felt if it had been me, if my mum had wanted to introduce another girl into the family when I was your age. Is it because Mum would like it to be a girl of around your age? Would you be happier if we were talking about a little boy, a brother for you?'

'I hate boys,' came my stiff, frozen robot voice.

'Or a baby.'

'Babies stink of poo,' I said.

Mum sighed, a deep, hopeless sigh, and I suddenly realised that I was the one with power now, not Molly, not Mum. I could make this thing not happen. They were waiting for me to say yes, and all I had to do was to say no. And when I realised that, I felt strong, my ice melted away from me and I went calmly upstairs to my room, put my magic twinkling shoes in their box, and started my maths homework.

I could hear Mum and Molly talking, their voices rolling and pattering and running together like rainwater. I wasn't upset any more, I wasn't angry. I just got on with what I wanted to do. No need to be cute and friendly and too nice to need a sister. After a bit, as I knew she would, Molly came up and knocked on my door. I didn't answer but she came in anyway and sat on the end of my bed. She tweaked her plait over her shoulder.

'Your mother and I have decided that I won't come again for a bit.'

Hmm. I finished my maths problem, closed the book, and clicked my pen so the nib retracted.

'Not unless you want me to,' Molly went on. 'Sharing your home with someone, adopting someone into it, is a really big decision, and the whole family really needs to want to do it. You're not at all sure about this. That's fine. Some children of your age feel puzzled. They think, why should Mum want another child, when she's got me?'

My breath gave a sharp snatch. I stared out of the window. The street was dark. The streetlamp was a hazy orange blur.

'Sometimes they feel jealous,' Molly went on quietly. 'They think, doesn't my mum love me? Aren't I enough for her?'

Just under my eyelids the tears were beginning to brim.

'Or they feel angry and upset.'

She was quiet for ages, and so was I. I could hear next door's dog padding down the entry, his paws scratching, whining at the gate to be let out.

'Does Mum really want to adopt someone?' I blurted it out, my eyes still on the blurry orange glow outside the window.

'Well, she does, very much.'

I swallowed hard. I didn't feel powerful any more. I felt little and hurt. 'Then she'd better do it, hadn't she?'

'No, not at all, not unless you want to. She's been thinking about this for a long time, but I know it's a new idea to you. It needs a lot of thinking about.'

I nodded, biting my lip, swallowing again.

'Some children say they don't even want to think about it again, and that's OK, that's the end of the matter.'

'What would you do, if I said that?'

'I'd go away and I promise I wouldn't come back to the house again, and Mum would know that that was the best thing to do.'

'I'll think about it,' I said.

She nodded, satisfied. 'I'm pleased,' she said. 'It would be a shame to dismiss the idea without thinking about it. Talk to your friends about it.'

I said nothing. Zeena was my only real friend, and she'd gone.

'I've brought something that might help you. You don't have to do this, but it sometimes helps.'

That was when Molly gave me the book. It was a large hardback book with pink and blue stripes across it.

I opened it up. The pages were completely blank, apart from faint grey lines. Molly rummaged in her bag again and gave me a gold plastic pen with 'zebra' written on the side.

'It might be a good idea to write all your thoughts down here,' she said. 'Just absolutely everything that comes into your head. You know, about your feelings, about your mum, about me if you want. You don't have to show it to anyone. Or you could show it to me one day, if you want to, and if you want me to come again. Some children write about their hobbies and their friends and their school too, but that's only when they decide that they want to adopt someone and they want to tell them about their family.'

'Like writing to a pen friend?'

'Mm, yes. That sort of thing.'

I stroked the book. 'Can I write about skating, even though we might not adopt anyone?'

'If you want. Gosh, that would be a lovely thing to write about.' Molly smiled and stood up. 'You'd enjoy that. But Rosa, only write the truth. OK? It isn't a storybook. OK?'

'OK,' I agreed.

Molly came over to where I was sitting and touched my cheek. 'I hope we meet again,' she said.

That night, I started to write in my book. I thought for ages about where to start it, and then I remembered the day Mum told me that she wanted us to adopt a sister. That was the day I had realised that I didn't know

Mum properly, that there was something about her that I didn't know and that I didn't understand. But I wasn't ready to go there yet. Instead, I wrote about skating.

I love skating, more than anything else in the world. Mum and I are learning together. We go to the skating rink every Saturday morning, and we take the same class. We're just about as good as each other. I can go backwards, I can spin, I can do cross-overs. I love the music, which makes me want to dance and sing, and the sounds of the skates freeshing on the ice. I love the rush of excitement I feel when I try a new move, and try and try again because it's too hard at first, testing out which way to tilt my foot, inside edge, outside edge, and then find out I can do it. Most of all, I love it because it's something my mum and I do together.

Once I'd started I just couldn't stop, it was pouring out of me, a river of words. At first everything came out in the wrong order, just as I remembered it. But now, I've reached the day where Molly gave me the striped book. I think I want to keep on writing in it. I'm trying to write the exact truth. And this is my true thought for today. I'm going to ask Mum why she wants another daughter.

9
ABELA

A month passed, and Abela slept a lot, cried a lot, dragged herself to school when she could. She kept thinking she could hear Mama singing, or the little whimpering cry that Nyota used to make when she was waking up, or her father's deep rolling laughter. But the little house was empty of sound, except for Bibi's low voice persuading her to eat, drink, get up, give her some help. It never occurred to Abela that her grandmother was as steeped in grief as she was for the three losses to her family. Bibi just kept going, and tried to keep the world moving for Abela.

One day when she came home from school, she found her grandmother making little maize cakes, special occasion cakes, on the griddle over the charcoal stove.

'I have had a message to say that your uncle is coming home!' Bibi's eyes were dancing with smiles. 'Yes, your Uncle Thomas has come home from Europe, and he has a surprise for you.'

'I don't know Uncle Thomas,' Abela said.

'Well, you do, but you were only four or five when he went away to Europe. He fell in love with a rich tourist who gave him the money to go to her country, and I thought he would never come home again.' She said the word *mzungu*, which meant tourist, with a mixture of pride and contempt. She did not like them. When they climbed off the bus to stretch their legs they stared and took photographs, they wandered round the village and peered in the huts as if they owned the place. Abela thought about the lady tourist with the hair like flames that she had met on the way to the hospital, and said nothing about it.

'Why has he come home from Europe?' she asked. To her, Europe was one big place, one massive world where many white people lived. Everybody who lived in Europe was rich. Why would Uncle Thomas want to come home again?

Bibi shrugged. She flipped the maize cakes over on the skillet. 'I know why, but I don't understand. He sent someone to tell me he was living in Dar es Salaam for a bit, and so I sent a message back on the bus to tell him about your mother. She was his sister. He needs to know that she has died. He needs to help us now. He has been trying to get the right papers to go back to England, something to do with that. He wasn't allowed to stay any longer.' She paused. 'They threw him out, his friend said,' she announced dramatically, as if that made him a hero.

Abela stared into the charcoal fire, frowning. She dimly remembered her uncle now. He was a bully, she remembered. He used to shout a lot at her mother, and sometimes he hit her. He used to tease Abela and chase her into the monkey woods until she cried, and then he would make his voice squawk like a hen with laughter. She used to be afraid of him.

'Well, he's coming home. I've had a message to say he will be on the bus tonight. All the way from Dar es Salaam! He'll be tired, he'll be hungry, he'll be dirty. Don't expect much from him tonight. He's bringing someone with him. And he has a surprise for you.'

'For me?'

'There, now you want to see him, don't you? He's a good boy. He doesn't forget his old mother and his little niece.'

When the cakes were made, Bibi shook out the bedroll ready for Uncle Thomas to sleep on. She and Abela would sleep together on Mama's bedroll, she said. Plenty of room. And the guest would sleep on Abela's bedroll. Bibi was like a girl again, excited and laughing at the thought of seeing her son after five years, and her excitement affected Abela. She magicked what the surprise might be in her head. Maybe he had brought her some pencils from Europe.

When the time came to meet the bus they strolled together through the compound and up past the schoolhouse to the road, Bibi shouting out to her friends that Thomas was coming home. The fireflies blazed a blue trail for them. Food stalls were being set up on trellis tables along the roadside to greet the bus passengers, paraffin lamps lit, music playing from someone's portable radio. Even though this happened every time the bus passed by the village, it felt as if everyone had turned out that night to meet Uncle Thomas.

The bus was five hours late. It didn't matter. That was

71

quite normal. Bibi chatted to the women at the stalls, sitting on the white plastic chair that one of the stallholders had brought home on a bus from Arusha. She teetered it backwards and forwards on three legs as she leaned round to talk, her hands flitting like bats, and Abela curled up on the ground and slept. The mad mzee prowled round, muttering to herself, her panga tucked under her arm till the Indian chilli-seller prised it away from her, chuckling softly. Abela heard the distant rumble of the bus as if it was inside her dream, and only woke up properly when she felt something tickling her cheek, and a woman's voice speaking to her. She opened her eyes to see a white woman looking down at her, the light of the lamps flickering across her face and making her long pale yellow hair gleam.

'What a pretty child, Thomas. Is this Bella?'

Recognising her name among the English words, Abela sat up with a start and struggled to her feet. Bibi was hugging Uncle Thomas, who was dressed in strange trousers and shoes, not blue jeans like the men in the village, not shorts like the tourists.

'Look at these smart clothes!' Bibi clucked in admiration. 'You must be a rich man these days!'

Thomas put his arm round his friend's waist. She swung her hair and gleamed a smile at him. 'This is Susie,' he said. 'Say hello, Abela. Say it in English.'

Abela rubbed the palms of her hands together nervously. 'Morning, Teacha!' she said.

'Well, it's not morning, it's nearly midnight,' Susie laughed. White, white, thought Abela. Oh, her voice is as white as the moon. I have never heard a lovely moon-white quiet-soft voice like that before. 'And I'm certainly not a teacher. Not clever enough! Not bossy enough!' She crouched down to Abela. 'Do you speak much English, Bella?'

Abela bit her lip and scratched the ground with her big toe. 'A little bit,' she whispered. She glanced shyly up at her grandmother. 'Teacha say me I best in school.' Then she burrowed her face into Bibi's side.

'You'd better be,' Susie said. 'Because I don't speak one word of your language. Oh, yes I do! One word – *jambo*! That means hello, doesn't it? I love that word. *Jambo*! *Jambo*, everybody!'

Bibi clicked her tongue in her cheek as if she were calling her cow to the end of her field for milking, and led the way towards the compound. She wanted to feed her guests before they slept, and that thought was far more important to her than talking to the pretty white woman her son had brought home. Abela struggled to stay awake while the bean stew and the maize cakes were prepared. The sky hung like a black tent over them. Susie and Thomas sat outside the hut with little lamps glowing around them to keep away the mosquitoes. Huge moths fluttered round the lamps and Susie flapped her hands at them. Her rings sparkled like stars. When Bibi proudly served out the bowls of food, Susie said she was too tired to eat.

'Can we go and sleep now?' she asked. 'I'm sorry, I can't keep my eyes open, Thomas.'

Thomas waved his hand towards his mother's hut. 'Go ahead.'

'In there? I can't sleep in there! Isn't there a hotel?'

'Not unless you want to walk about fifty miles.'

Bibi smiled and nodded, understanding nothing except that her guest was too tired to eat.

Susie peered into the hut, and backed out again. 'I won't sleep in there,' she said firmly. 'It's too dark, and it stinks of smoke, and there's no room.'

'Oh, for heaven's sake!' Thomas snapped.

'Isn't there a proper house anywhere?'

'Stop whining! If you're tired, sleep in there. If you're not, sit here and wait for the lions.'

Susie yelped and groped her way into the blackness of the mud hut, and Bibi followed her and showed her the bedroll that she was to sleep on. Susie covered herself up with the blanket and went straight to sleep. Abela lay on the roll that used to be Mama's and looked across at her, at the beautiful pale yellow hair, at the white face like a sleeping moon, just lit by the glow from outside.

The fire under the cooking pot died down, the hut was in darkness, and still Bibi and Uncle Thomas talked on, sitting just outside the hut in the starlight. He told his mother about the house he had lived in when he was in England, with a room for every person, a kitchen full of things that worked by electricity and a bathroom with running hot water.

'I have heard that the people in Dar and Arusha and

Moshi live like that,' Bibi said, not impressed. 'All the big towns.'

'Only the rich ones, Mama. In England, everybody does. Everybody. They all have cars! They have computers, they have mobile phones. Everybody.'

'Tchk! What are these things anyway? Where you going to live, now you're back here?'

'I'm not staying here. This is no place for a man to live, not when I've seen how rich people live. I'm going back to England as soon as I get my papers.'

'What are these papers?'

'Immigration papers. Well, Mama,' and he lowered his voice, 'I got into BIG trouble with the officials there because I only went for a holiday and I stayed for five years! They didn't like that!' He laughed his squawking-hen laugh. In the hut, Susie murmured softly in her sleep. 'I didn't have a work permit, Mama, that's all. It's nothing.'

'I talked to the teacher yesterday,' Bibi said. 'She told me, it's bad news that they threw you out. Once you're out, you're out, she said. They won't want you back.' Her voice was greedy with love; after all, she wanted her son to stay home with her.

'They'll want me all right. I have a plan.' He turned round and looked back at the dark sleeping shape of Susie. 'They won't want to keep me away from my wife and child.'

'Your wife? You married to this woman?'

'Not yet. Tomorrow, next day.'

75

'What about that girl from long ago, who took you away with her?'

'Oh, her!' Thomas grinned at his mother. 'She was rich, but she was stupid! We didn't get on.'

'Tchk! So you found another one. Well, she's prettier than the first. And she's having your baby?'

'She was, Mama. Then she lost him before he was born. The baby died.' His voice grew bitter and angry. 'But I have a plan. I told you. I have a plan, and they won't stop me going back to England now.'

In the long silence that followed, Abela drifted off to sleep, and never heard what her Uncle Thomas's plan might be.

As soon as she woke up, she remembered that Susie was there. She sat up and looked across to where the pink morning light lit up Susie's face and hair. She could see the fine golden down on her cheeks, and the flutter of her pale eyelashes. Bibi was stoking the stove to heat up the maize porridge for breakfast, and a sudden gust of smoke drenched the air. Susie woke up, coughing. She blundered outside, gasping and spluttering, breathing in the fresh air.

'How can you live in there, with all that smoke?' she shouted. 'I smell like a kipper, Thomas.'

Thomas stretched and rolled himself over. 'You get used to it,' he called back. 'Don't make a fuss.'

But Abela jumped out of her bedroll and ran to the red plastic bucket of water that Bibi had carried from the well the day before, balancing it on her head the way all the women did, never spilling a drop all the long way home. She scooped some out with a coconut shell and carried it over to where Susie sat, still gasping, away from the house.

Susie shook her head. 'You're a good girl,' she said. 'But I daren't drink this water. I'll get typhoid or something. I've got some in a bottle somewhere in my bag.'

'It very good water,' Abela said, understanding a little. She sipped some and offered the shell bowl again. 'Mm, good for Susie. *Mimi ninapenda*. Very nice.'

Uncle Thomas strolled over to them, his shirt loose over his strange trousers. He was carrying a plastic bottle of water and a bowl of maize porridge. He squatted down beside them. 'What do you think of Abela? Is she good enough? Smile, Abela. Smile for Susie.'

Abela bit her lip, wishing he would go away and leave her with Susie.

'She's just lost her mother, poor kid. Why should she smile?' Susie said. 'She's lovely. Anyway, what do you mean, good enough? Good enough for what?'

Thomas didn't answer. He told Abela to fetch some porridge for herself and Susie, and laughed at the face Susie pulled when she tasted it.

'How old are you, Abela?' he asked suddenly, in English.

'I think I nine year old,' Abela answered proudly.

'She's little for her age,' he commented. He dug his fingers into Abela's shoulders, turning her round and

77

sizing her up as if she were a calf he might be buying from the market. He cupped her face in his hands. 'Skinny as a rat. Open your mouth,' he ordered. 'Baby teeth, still.'

She pulled away from him, her eyes stinging, and he laughed and tweaked her nose playfully.

'Are you going to school today?' he asked.

Abela nodded. She didn't want to. She wanted to stay and look at Susie all day.

'Take Susie with you, show her round. She'd like to meet your teacher. She can talk some new English words to you kids. And afterwards, take her to the market.' He fished in his pockets and tossed some coins on the ground. 'Buy your grandmother some decent cakes, and a kuku, a nice fat chicken. And get yourself a nice new kanga to wear at my wedding. You too, Susie.' He added in English. 'I want you to wear a kanga tomorrow.'

'It'll make me look too pale. They're all such bright colours, Thomas,' Susie reminded him, pretending to pout. She stood up, stretching, combing her hair back with her fingers. 'God, I could do with a hair wash. I must look like a tramp.'

'You look beautiful. Doesn't she, Abela?' Thomas poked Abela.

'You very nice,' Abela said shyly. She covered her face with her hands and giggled.

'Thank you. OK, I'd like to see your school, Bella. Will you show me?'

She stood up and held out her hand, and Abela took it

in her own. The eyes of all the village were on her as she walked hand in hand with the beautiful white stranger to the schoolhouse, and she kept her lips bunched, just a little, in imitation of the pretty pout that Susie had made.

As soon as they were out of sight, Thomas called his mother over. 'Has the kid been to the clinic recently? Have they tested her for HIV?'

'She's clear,' Bibi said. 'We're both clear, thanks be to Jesus Christ our Lord.'

'She's had all the tests? You're quite sure? She's had injections? You got the papers to show me?' he demanded.

'They gave me something. How do I know what it says?' His mother went into the hut, lifted up the bedroll that Thomas had been sleeping on, and brought out a document. He scrutinised it carefully and then folded it and put it in his back pocket.

'How do you think you're going back to that place, England? Tell me about this plan of yours,' his mother said.

Thomas laughed. He took some coins from his pocket and juggled them up and down in the palm of his hand. 'In a few days, Susie has to return to England. She's already bought her ticket, so she has to go then. But when she goes back, she'll be married to me.' He tiptoed a dance around his mother, a stately Western dance, jingling the coins like bells and making her smile. 'I get the documents tomorrow. Then I just have to apply to join my wife. That's what my plan is.'

'I don't understand. What documents? All documents, papers, this and that, passports, I don't understand any of it.' The old woman flapped her hand in front of her face as if she were flapping flies away. 'And how can you get married tomorrow? Tomorrow is not the priest's day for coming here.'

'Priest!' Thomas laughed. 'I don't need a priest!' He drew a wad of bank notes out of his pocket. 'This is all I need. American dollars. More valuable than English sterling. I can buy anything I want with these, if I give them to the right people. I can buy a marriage certificate. I can buy a paper to say we have a child.'

'Your child was never born. You told me.'

'No problem. I can buy a certificate to say I have a daughter. A birth certificate. The English government won't keep me away from my wife and child. I can buy a passport for her.'

'For her? For whom?' His mother sat down suddenly on the little stool she used for shredding coconut. She knew, of course she knew, whom he was talking about, but her quaking heart would not allow her to say so.

'For Abela Mbisi.' He bent down to her, smiling, and whispered the words in her ear.

'My Abela?'

'Your Abela! My dead sister's orphan child, in need of a mother and father. What kind of a life will she have here? How long can you look after her? When I have these papers, it will say that Abela is my daughter, Susie's daughter. It will say she is seven years old. That will sound better – Susie's only twenty-five. So, Abela goes home to England with her mother at the end of the week. And I will apply for immigration papers because I have a wife and child in England. It's so simple. You have a clever son, Mother.' He went down on his knees and put his arms round her. 'You want this for me, don't you? You want it for Abela. A better life, away from all this poverty and disease? When I'm back in England I can get a job. I know how to earn good money, very, very good money. And everything I earn I'll send to you. Half.'

'Tchk! Money! What do I want with money!' His mother swiped his arms away. 'I won't let you take Abela away from me. She's all I've got.'

Thomas stood up again and shook the dust from the knees of his trousers. 'And you're a selfish old cow. In England she'll have shoes on her feet and good food in her belly. She'll sleep in a big house and go to a proper school. She'll get a good education. She'll get good medical care. I'm offering her the chance of a lifetime. Ma, listen to me. I know about these things. There are other little girls that I have found homes for – I know nice English families who want little girls like Abela to help them in their big house. There's plenty money for you and me.' He rubbed his thumb and first finger together. 'And plenty good life for my sister's child. Who are you to turn it down for her?'

'She won't want to leave me,' Bibi muttered. 'She loves her grandmother.'

'She loves Susie already. You saw them, hand in hand. They're getting on like a house on fire.'

'A house on fire!' His mother was horrified. 'What a terrible thought.'

The next day, Abela wore her new yellow and black kanga and Susie wore a red and green one that Abela had chosen for her in the market. They walked solemnly behind Uncle Thomas to the next village, where they met two strangers in a concrete schoolhouse. One of the men talked in rapid Kiswahili, which Thomas translated for Susie. The other man, glistening with sweat, sat at a desk and wrote meticulously on three pieces of paper. Abela noticed that he didn't use a pencil, but a black pen with a gold nib. From time to time he shook it to make the ink flow. When he had finished writing, he asked Uncle Thomas and Susie for their signatures. Then he produced a camera and ushered them outside, and took photographs, one of the group together, one of Thomas on his own, one of Susie with Abela, one of Thomas with Abela, and one with Abela on her own.

'Smile!' Uncle Thomas shouted. 'Look happy! It's my wedding day.' He looked at the other men and squawked with laughter. Abela was too frightened to smile. Nothing like this had ever happened to her before. What happened to her when the camera was pointed at her like that? She had heard that it took your soul away, to have a photograph taken. She clutched her arms across her chest, holding her soul in place.

'That should cover all possibilities,' Abela heard the man with the camera say to her uncle. 'That's done now.'

Both men shook hands with Thomas and Susie and pronounced them married.

'Is that it?' Susie asked doubtfully. 'Is that how you do it here?'

'It is when you're in a hurry,' Thomas told her. He kissed her hand, which was melting with sweat by now. 'We'll do it again when I'm home in England with you. You can have a church wedding and a white dress like a fairy, and a taxi to the church, and a big party.' He spoke to her as if she were a little girl deserving treats for being good.

Susie frowned, knowing that that was unlikely too. Her parents didn't like Thomas at all. They'd met him twice, when they had visited her in London, and they had told her then to keep clear of him.

'He's using you, Susie. Promise me you won't marry him. All he wants is a British passport. It's not you he's interested in,' her mother had warned her.

'He loves me,' Susie insisted.

'He loves your blonde hair, that's all,' said her mother cynically. 'I know you love him, but that's a different thing altogether. I don't want you to be hurt.'

So she didn't tell her parents when Thomas was deported from England because he had stayed without a visa, an illegal immigrant. She was very much in love with him. She couldn't bear to be without him, so she agreed to go with him to Tanzania to be married. She simply told her parents that she was going on a long holiday because she needed a break from her work. She didn't tell them, either, that she was going to have his baby, or that she had miscarried at five months. She thought she was going to lose Thomas then, too, because he seemed to lose interest in her at that point. But coming to Tanzania with him had brought them closer together. And then when he said he wanted to marry her, all she could think of was that he loved her after all. What would her mother think now of this bleak little ceremony in a concrete hut, in a language she didn't understand, with only a little girl as a witness? She watched Thomas as he brought out some bank notes and handed them to the men.

'Is that usual too?' she asked, doubtful again.

'I've told you, we're in a hurry. And these men have come a long way. You don't expect them to do it for nothing, do you? If you didn't have to go back, we would have had more time. But how could I let you go back to England without marrying you? I love you too much for that.'

He kissed her then, and Abela, hovering behind Susie, lowered her eyes and smiled. She still didn't like her uncle much, but she already loved his princess bride. She didn't know yet about the plan to send her to England. Her grandmother was too upset to tell her. Her uncle wasn't sure that her forged passport would be ready in time, so he said nothing. And as for Susie, she simply didn't know.

• • •

After the wedding, Uncle Thomas went off somewhere with the two men. He told Susie he was going to sort out his documents. The three men walked away, laughing, Thomas in the middle with his arms over the shoulders of the other two. Abela saw them heading for the local pombe bar where a strong beer made of coconut palm sap was sold, but she said nothing. She knew her mother had hated that place where men liked to go for hours on end, often shouting and silly by the time they came home. Bibi hated it too. There was no reason to suppose that Susie would want to go there with him. So they walked back to Bibi's house hand in hand. Boys tending their goats in an overgrown cemetery shouted greetings to them. High above their heads men were working in the trees collecting honey, singing loudly. Monkeys jabbered a shrill chorus. A laughing jackass cackled down at them. It was a day like any other day, but it should have been a special day. Abela could sense that Susie was sad; she wanted to make her smile again.

'Tell me English,' she said.

Susie laughed, a strange, dry, choked laugh with no sunshine in it. 'Today is my wedding day,' she said. 'Your Uncle Thomas is my husband. Do you understand that, Abela?'

'No,' said Abela, trying to pout.

'Neither do I,' said Susie. 'All I want is to go back home with Thomas, and be happy.'

'Happy,' said Abela. 'I know the word happy.'

'Are you happy, Abela?'

'No,' Abela said. 'No Mama. No happy.'

Bibi had made them a wedding feast of beans and chillies cooked with bananas and rice, and a special pudding of mangoes cooked in coconut milk. She was angry when she saw that Thomas wasn't with them.

'Where's he gone?' she asked Abela. 'To the pombe, I suppose.'

'He's getting the documents,' Abela said.

'Tchk! Documents!'

They waited till after dark for Thomas to come, and when he didn't come they ate without him, sitting outside around the charcoal fire so the smoke inside the hut wouldn't make Susie cough. The stars were huge and brilliant, the frogs and the insects were singing loudly and brightly.

'The stars are like showers of spray from a fountain! It's a beautiful night,' said Susie softly, aloud, even though Bibi couldn't understand. 'And this is a beautiful country. But oh! I'm longing to go back to England. Home.'

'Home,' repeated Abela, knowing the word.

It was morning before Thomas came back, neither shouting nor silly, but deeply angry. Abela was giving Susie a cookery lesson. Susie was perched on a tiny wooden stool, twisting a coconut round the little serrated knife attached to it.

'This stool is called *mbuzi*,' Abela told Susie. 'It has same name as goat.'

'Boozy,' Susie laughed. 'That's what my husband is, I'm afraid! Where are you, you boozy goat?'

'You scrape the coconut, and I catch in clay pot. Now we squeeze with our hands, like this, all juice come out.'

'With my hands! Oh yuck! My mother would have a fit if she saw me doing this!'

They were laughing together, concentrating deeply, when Thomas walked into the compound. 'Look, Mister Goat! We're making coconut sauce!' Susie shouted. He ignored her and went straight to his mother.

'I can't get a passport for Abela. She can't leave when Susie does,' he told her. He paced round her, kicking angrily at the skinny cat who was mewing round their feet for the coconut milk. 'They're idiots, those men. They said they knew someone who could find me one in time.'

His mother clicked her tongue. 'It is not good to do things this way,' she said. 'It is not lawful.'

'Who cares about the law!'

'What's the matter?' Susie asked.

'Nothing,' he told her. 'Just some hold up with the travel documents.'

'What documents?' Susie asked. 'I've got my passport, it's OK. We are properly married, aren't we, Thomas?'

'Hey, I tell you, we're mister and missus now!' He pulled the signed marriage certificate out of the back pocket of his trousers to show her, and another paper fell to the floor. Susie bent to pick it up, and read the words before Thomas had time to snatch it away from her.

'HIV?' There was a frightened, frozen silence. Susie's

87

face had gone very white. 'HIV? HIV/Aids? What does this mean? Aids? Why have you got these papers?'

'It's just a certificate my mother got for Abela. I'll tell you on the bus, OK?'

But Susie's breath was coming in quick, sharp gasps. She backed away from Thomas. 'Are you telling me these people have Aids? And I've been sleeping here? I've been eating and sleeping with people who have Aids?'

'They don't have Aids. These are papers to show they *don't* have Aids.' His voice was low and reasoning, pushed out between his teeth, urging her to be calm and quiet. Pimples of sweat were breaking out on his forehead.

'Is that what your sister died of? Aids?' Susie's voice was rising to a pitch of hysteria. 'It is, isn't it? Why didn't you tell me? You bring me here, knowing all this?'

Realising that Susie was upset, but not knowing the reason for it, Abela ran to her, wanting to put her arms round her pale princess, but that made Susie panic even more.

'Keep away from me!' she shouted. 'Don't touch me. Go away.'

It was impossible for Thomas to calm her down. Susie refused to go back into Bibi's house again, convinced that she would catch Aids if she touched anything belonging to them. Abela and her grandmother stood together, bewildered and frightened, understanding nothing of what was going on, of the white fury that had taken possession of Susie. In the end Thomas took Susie to the teacher's house, which wasn't a round mud

88

hut like his mother's but a concrete building with four rooms. He asked Mrs Long to explain to Susie that she couldn't catch Aids by sleeping in the house where HIV/Aids victims had lived, and to show her the documents that testified that his mother and Abela were clear of the deadly disease. In spite of all Mrs Long's reassurances, Susie was still too upset and afraid to go back to Bibi's house. In the end the teacher said she could stay there with her until the time came for her to leave for the airport at Dar es Salaam.

'She stays with me,' Thomas insisted. 'She's my wife.'

'Is this true?' the teacher asked Susie. Along with the entire village, she knew all about Thomas Mkumba's expulsion from England. She also knew that it meant that it was very unlikely that he would ever be able to return there, though he boasted freely that he would soon be going back and that he would be a rich man in no time.

'We were married yesterday,' Susie said.

Mrs Long frowned. 'Are you sure about this?' she asked.

'Of course we're sure. We love each other,' said Susie, completely misunderstanding her.

'We have the papers,' said Thomas, understanding her completely.

'Papers,' the teacher sighed. 'I hope it's all right. I hope you'll be happy,' she said. 'And I hope it's what you really want, Susie,' she added, silently.

• • •

They both stayed at Mrs Long's that night. In their plain room, an electric fan whirred into the sweaty heat. Susie nervously watched the lizards scurrying across the ceiling. She had had enough. All she wanted now was to go home. Coming to Africa had been a big mistake. It had been all right in the cities and big towns, where streets were lit at night and the traffic and big shops and the stylish clothes were comfortingly familiar, where all the hotels had air conditioning. She didn't understand the people in these mud hut villages, these people who seemed to live on nothing at all, no domestic comfort, yet could still smile and gossip and sing. She wondered how on earth a woman like Mrs Long could have chosen to make her home there.

Thomas made quite sure that the two women had no time to talk together. He had no intention of letting Mrs Long express her doubts to Susie about the validity of the marriage papers. The sooner Susie got home, the better; then he could begin his plea to join her in England.

The next morning they left for Dar es Salaam. Bibi and Abela went to the bus station to say goodbye to them; Bibi gave Abela a little basket made of banana leaves to give to Susie. Abela was fretful, keeping her head down, not daring to look at Susie in case she started shouting at her again. When Susie crouched down to smile weakly at her she felt as if the world had started turning again.

'Please don't go home,' she said. She had practised the English words all the way to the bus stop.

'You be a good girl. Help your grandma,' Susie said. She ferreted in her bag and brought out a little key chain made of coloured beads, with a tiny mirror dangling on the end of it. 'Here. This is for you, Bella.'

'Look, look, Bibi!' Abela gasped. 'Look what Susie has given me!'

Her grandmother turned it over in her fist. The little mirror flashed and sparkled, catching winks of blue sky and dithering leaves in its glass.

'Do you like Susie?' Uncle Thomas asked casually.

Abela flung her arms wide open and danced round Susie. 'I love her! I love her this much!'

'I'll sort the passport out when I'm in Dar,' Thomas told his mother. 'We'll have to send the kid over on her own, then I'll get my own visa sorted out. Meanwhile, get her clean. You know what I mean, Mama. And get that teacher to give her extra English lessons. It'll be easier for her that way.'

He climbed on the bus after Susie. Abela ran alongside, waving, and Susie, pale and still upset, full of misgivings, waved back. Only when the bus had completely disappeared from sight, and the roar of its engine had disappeared, would Abela agree to go to school with her grandmother.

'So you like that lady, Uncle Thomas's wife?' Bibi asked as they waited together to speak to Mrs Long.

'Yes,' said Abela. 'She's very pretty. I wish she would stay here with us.'

Bibi nodded. Maybe Thomas was right. Maybe it was

91

selfish of her to want to keep Abela in the village without a mother and father. What was there for her here?

'How good is Abela's English?' she asked Mrs Long.

'Very good,' the teacher smiled. 'She's a very clever girl. She learns very fast.'

'Does she?' Bibi's heart was big with pride. 'Give her lots of English words, Teacha. She's going to live in England with her new mother and father.' She looked down at Abela's startled face. 'There,' she said. 'Now you know, Abela. Now you have your Uncle Thomas's surprise.'

10
ROSA

I don't know why it took me so long to ask Mum that big question. I've practised it many times on my own, looking out of my window at the frost skin on the grass, at the little grey sparrows shivering on the bird table. Sometimes, even though it's so cold, I open the window and breathe the words out into the spiky air. They hang there for a second, and then they float away with the specks of tiny snowflakes. And so, instead, I write them down in the stripy book that Molly gave me.

I really enjoy writing in the stripy book. It feels as if I'm talking to someone close. It feels as if I've been getting to know myself, like when I was little and I used to stand on tiptoe to see myself in the mirror in the bathroom, glass finger touching glass nose. I've told the book lots of things that I've never told anyone else. I've even drawn sketches of me on the skating rink, Mum on the rink, Molly and her shoes. I think it was all avoidance tactics really, because the first and most important thing, the big WHY, has been there at the front of my mind all the time, like a big hovering bird, like the kestrels we see when we're driving on the motorway. Maybe I'm scared of what I might catch, that's why I don't swoop down and strike. I'm scared of what Mum's answer might be.

'You're not good enough, Rosa,' she might say. 'I wanted a different kind of daughter.' She might. We're not a bit alike, Mum and I. We don't look alike, we don't act alike. But I needed to know, didn't I? I had to.

So I waited for the right moment, like the wind-hovering kestrel waits for the little mouse to scuttle out of hiding and just sit there, whiskers quivering, enjoying the sunshine. Pounce.

The trouble is, Mum never stops. She's got restless hands and itchy feet, Nana says. She's always busy. She's never just sitting there, relaxed and smiling, waiting for me to ask her something important. So what I did was this: I made the moment happen. I took down the teddy-bear curtains from my bedroom and plonked them on the kitchen table.

'Oh,' Mum said, frowning. 'Do they need washing?'

'They need throwing,' I said. 'I don't know if you've noticed, but I'm thirteen and a quarter years old these days.'

'Right. Well, I had noticed, because you've suddenly become utterly gorgeous, but I'd stopped noticing the curtains. I'll wash them and take them to Oxfam. Some cute seven-year-old will love them.'

We started to take the plastic hooks out together, and that was when I took a deep breath and blurted it out.

'Mum. Why do you want to adopt another girl?'

Then *she* took a deep breath and fiddled with her impossible hair for a second, scooping it back behind her ears. 'Not just any other girl, Rosa. I want her to come from Tanzania.'

And that set my head reeling, and I felt like the kestrel must feel when it's caught its prey and suddenly lifts up and soars away towards the sun. It just shows, doesn't it, if you don't ask, you don't find out. I might never have known.

'You didn't tell me.'

'Well, Molly and I agreed that it wasn't what you needed to know, not at first. You needed to get used to the idea of adopting a sister at first. Of including a new person in the family. That was what we really needed to talk to each other about. But you really didn't want to. You didn't want to talk about the idea at all. So Molly and I agreed not to pursue it.'

That's what she said, and that really was the answer to the question, and it was all I wanted to know at that moment. I needed to go upstairs and think about it. I needed to write it all down in the stripy book. It really did explain everything.

And this is the reason: I'm black. I'm from Tanzania. Although I'm British, I was born in Africa.

And my mum is white.

Later, after tea, after I'd done my homework and had my bath, I came down in my red winter jim-jams and snuggled up to Mum. She was writing a report of some kind, but she put it down straight away and looped her arm round my shoulder.

95

'Mum,' I said, 'tell me about Baba.'

Baba is what my mum always calls my father. She says it means Daddy in Swahili, which is strange of course, because you'd expect it to mean baby.

'You know all about Baba,' she laughed, and she was pleased, I could tell; pleased to be talking about him, pleased to be with me, cosy on the settee again like we used to be. So was I.

'Tell me again. I want to know again.' I know the story of Baba of course. But I know it from long ago, like I know the story of *Snow White* or *Hansel and Gretel*. Once upon a time, in a country far away ...

'I went to Tanzania when I was about thirty. I'd been teaching for a few years, and I wanted a change of scenery. I wanted to do something really useful and important before I settled down. I wanted to go to Africa! And I managed to do all those things when I applied to do VSO, which means Voluntary Service Overseas, helping people in developing countries. It was exactly what I wanted to do. And they gave me a job teaching in a little Tanzanian town called Korogwe.'

'Korogwe,' I repeated. It was a magical name to me, like Transylvania or Arabia. A story name.

'I loved it there,' Mum said. 'It was such a rich place – I don't mean rich in money, far from it. But the people were so warm and friendly, and the land was so fertile, and the colours everywhere were so vivid – huge bright butterflies, and trees like flames – and everywhere you look, wild flowers as bright as jewels. There's nowhere like it. If I think about it now, I can smell it. Sharp, sweet, tomatoey smell. I can taste the little bananas they have there, lovely juicy, lemony, fat bananas, in great swathes on the market stalls. I can hear the voices of the children in the school – "Mornin', Teacha!" they used to shout, any time of day, whenever they saw me riding my bike round the town! I can hear the singing of the frogs, and I can see the blue glimmer of fireflies at night, and the stars, Rosa, stars as thick as a field of daisies in the sky.'

'And the moon is upside down, like a boat.'

'Hm-hm. I fell in love with Korogwe, and when I met Baba, I fell in love with him, too. He was tall and very, very handsome. He was brought up on the Maasai Plain, where the mountains are like purple cones and the earth is beautiful with African violets. He belonged to the Maasai tribe, who are usually nomadic people, cattle herders. They're very beautiful people, slim, strong and powerful. The men wear deep red robes and have bangles round their ankles and beads round their necks and dangling from their ears. And the women wear purple, and sometimes they cover their heads with a rich orange ochre. They're so graceful, the Maasai. So proud and graceful.'

I loved to hear this. These were my people that Mum was talking about. My family. 'Is that what Baba looked like when you met him?'

'Well, not really. Not the earrings and bangles. When he was about your age he met some priests and they

97

took him to a town called Arusha to study with the Jesuits. He was an excellent student. They sent him on to university and he studied politics and philosophy; he was such a clever man. He could have done anything with his life, but when I met him he was training to be a teacher at a seminary. He wanted to be a missionary, to help his own people.'

The phone rang shrilly, interrupting the story that was the story of my life. We both started, but Mum pulled me closer and chose to ignore the phone. The answerphone message droned as we carried on.

'But instead, he met you and fell in love. Was that wrong of him?'

'Not wrong, but not right either. When you fall in love with someone it's really hard to behave rationally. You'll understand that one day, Rosa. It's hard to see beyond the moment into the future. We saw each other as much as we could, and after a year, I fell pregnant. You were born in the clinic there. My beautiful baby. Nobody knew who your father was; I kept it secret. After all, he was going to be a teacher; maybe even a priest. My contract with VSO was over; I had to come home, and I really did want to come home by then. I was terribly homesick. I wanted my family to see my beautiful baby; I needed my mum! And so Baba agreed to come with me. It was a huge sacrifice for him – he was giving up his training, he was giving up Africa!'

When she said *Africa* it always made me think of a black rose blooming open to show all its golden and yellow and red heart colours. I lost myself then, and so did she, and there was only Twitchy, flicking her ear and muttering cattish dream thoughts to make any sound in the room at all. Then Mum fished in her pocket for a tissue and blew her nose, and carried on.

'So we came home, you, me and Baba, and we lived at my mum and dad's.'

She paused again. The electric fire flickered its dance of pretend flames across her face. Her eyes gleamed.

'But he hated it here,' I prompted her.

'He did. He hated wearing shoes all the time, he hated the noise of the traffic and the bustle of the streets. Even though his mission house had been in Arusha, which is a big town, he couldn't get used to Sheffield. He hated the cold. He hated the rain and the fog. He hated the food and the carpets and the furniture. He hated shopping in supermarkets. He was like a bird trapped in a cage. He stopped singing. He stopped smiling. And one day my handsome black prince just left, just like that. He didn't leave a message. But his passport had gone, and his tribal clothes that he wore in the house, and I knew that he had flown home like a migrating bird.'

'And we never saw him again.'

'No, my love. He sent me a letter from Tanzania telling me that he still loved me and he loved you, very much, but that his heart was in Africa. He still wanted to be a priest, and the mission house had agreed to take him back. He still wanted to work for his own people.

His ambition was that one day he would be sent to work in one of the poorest countries in Africa, somewhere like Rwanda. He hoped I would understand and that one day, you would too.'

Do I? I think I do.

Actually, I love the story of my mum and Baba. I don't mind that he lives in Africa. I'm used to just living with Mum. Lots of times kids at school ask me why it is that I'm black and my mother is white and I tell them I'm mixed race, dual culture. I'm proud to tell them that my father is a black prince from the Maasai Plain. But from today, if I'm asked again, I'll tell them that he is a priest working to help his own people.

'So, to answer your question,' Mum went on. 'Why do I want to adopt another girl? Well, I think it would be wonderful for you to have a Tanzanian sister. I've always thought that, though it's taken me a long time to realise that adoption is the only way that this can happen. I'm never going to live in Tanzania again, much as I love it. This is my home. And I just feel now is the right time.' She pushed her hair behind her ears; I know when she does that it's because she has important things to say. 'It's not easy to get accepted as an adoptive mother though.'

'Have you been accepted?' I asked.

'No.'

'Was it because I didn't want to adopt?'

'Yes, Rosa, it was. We had to be accepted as a family.'

She went out to the kitchen to make a drink. Long

past my bedtime, and she hadn't told me to go up yet. I was nearly ready. I followed her into the kitchen.

'Mum, can you ask Molly to come again?' I said. 'I really, really want us to adopt. I really, really do.'

11
ABELA

It was two months before Abela's passport arrived, and during that time she heard nothing from Susie, her white princess, or from Uncle Thomas. She thought Bibi must have been mistaken, and secretly she didn't care either. Why should she have to go to Europe when everything she loved was here? She didn't even know what it meant, to live in Europe, to go to Europe. How far away was it, and what was it like, and how did you get there? Did you walk? She didn't know, and she didn't ask. But she took extra lessons in English from Mrs Long, and didn't mind that at all. Mrs Long told her stories about her own childhood, when she lived in a big city in the north of England, and went to school with hundreds of other children.

'Is England a very nice place?' Abela asked her.

'Sometimes. Parts of it are very beautiful. Sometimes it's very ugly. Some people can make places ugly.'

'Is that why you live here?'

'Mostly, yes. It suits me. It's very beautiful here. And so are the people.'

Abela frowned. She understood all the words, but not the ideas. How could people make places ugly?

'I like it here too,' she said at last. 'I don't want to go somewhere ugly.'

During that time, a cousin came to tell Bibi that Abela's aunties in her old village had died of HIV/Aids. Bibi grieved again; all her daughters were dead now. Was there no end to it all? The priest asked the villagers to pray for the sick. 'It is not just here,' he told them. 'This is a disease that has spread all over Africa. In other countries it is far, far worse than anything we have seen. All over the world, people suffer from this thing.'

Women from the village came to each household to talk about protection from Aids. It was all more than Abela could understand.

'Will we all die?' she asked Bibi, and the terror of the thought kept her awake at night. Whenever she thought about it she felt as if she was letting go of herself; she felt as if she was spinning in a vast lonely black sky, with no stars, no moon, nothing but blackness. Bibi would hear her struggling to wake herself out of nightmares and would hug Abela close to her, folding her in her arms, rocking her.

'Sssh, baby, sssh. You're quite safe. This country is cursed now, that's what my friends tell me. It's not our faults, we're not bad people. What did we do wrong? We work hard and we pray and we look after each other. And still we get sick, and when we are sick, there's not enough medicine to help us. But when Thomas takes you away from here, I'll be happy for you.' She clasped Abela's face in her hands. 'I'll have to get you ready, so that when he comes, you can go.'

• • •

And one day soon after that my Bibi who loves me so much did to me the thing that gave me so much pain that I thought I was going to die. She woke me up early and she said, 'Abela, today we have to get you clean. We have to get you ready for when Thomas comes.'

At first I don't understand what she means when she says this. Mrs Long is getting me ready to go to an English school by teaching me lots of English words. Bibi can't do this. The priest is getting me ready for my first Holy Communion by teaching me the catechism. *Who made you? God made me. Why did God make you? God made me to know Him, love Him and serve Him.* We chant all the pages of the catechism every Sunday after church until I know all the words, and he says I am ready. So I look at her, puzzled, and I know it is nothing to do with my English words or my catechism, but that she is full of some deep secret, and her face is smiling though her eyes are tight and dark. She says, 'You are nine years old, Abela. I can't let you leave this village until you are ready. You'll see. You must be clean before you go.'

I am still puzzled, and I am a little afraid now. Then she tells me that she has sent for the medicine woman to come from another village, and then I know as much as I have ever known. I have heard the whispers when girls go away from my school and sometimes don't come back for weeks, and when they come back they walk like old women for a time, as if their bodies and

104

their legs are separate things. And sometimes they don't come back at all. They are never seen again. The hyenas have taken them, the village women say. These are things that I have known all my life, things that I am so afraid of that I cannot think about them, cannot believe they could happen to me, that my beautiful, kind, loving Bibi would do these things to me.

Bibi and her friend come to find me when I am playing with my Coca-Cola car in the ditch. They come and call my name and stand with their arms folded, waiting, and I know that my time has come and I am weak and trembling with fear. I want my mother. At first I pretend not to hear them but the air is beating wildly round my head like the wings of angels and I know I have to do what they tell me to do. They take me gently by each arm but I am still clutching my car. They take me down to the red fire tree at the bottom of Bibi's field, and there the old medicine woman is waiting.

She has a knife and she is sharpening it on a stone. I have to lie down on the earth and Bibi puts her hand over my mouth so I won't scream. I look up at her and she is watching me with shame and love and pity and pain and all these thoughts in her eyes seem to go back hundreds and hundreds of years. The angel wings are beating so fast around me that I have lost myself.

When I wake up, I am in Bibi's hut. The pain between my legs where the medicine woman cut me is so sharp that I want to scream, but the screaming is in my head, and the only sound I make is a whimper like the little mew that kittens make. Bibi comes to me and takes my hand and says, 'Good girl. Now you are clean, Abela. Now you can be a woman.'

It is days before I can walk again, and then I can only hobble, pressing my thighs together. I feel the knife pain again every time my water comes between my legs. I think the pain will last for ever. I think I will die of it. But by the time Uncle Thomas comes for me, I am healed. Now I am clean. But when was I dirty?

She saw Uncle Thomas coming from the bus, but because he was on his own this time she didn't run to him. She squatted down with the younger children, head bent so he wouldn't see her. She had a toy car made out of a Coca-Cola tin, red and silver. Her father had made it for her years ago, and now all the children had made copies of it and scooted them up and down the narrow runs they had channelled out in the yellow earth. Hers was still the best.

Her grandmother called her to the house and reluctantly she picked up her car and ran home. Her uncle scooped her up and tried to kiss her, but she swung her head away so his lips only touched her ear. He dropped her to the ground and she landed on all fours, like a cat.

'Get her ready,' he told his mother. 'We're going back on tomorrow's bus. She's flying from Dar tomorrow night.'

'Tomorrow!' Bibi wailed. She folded her skinny arms across her chest, rocking herself backwards and forwards. 'Not so soon! I'm to lose my little girl so soon?' She clutched out at Abela's hand. 'Will I see her again? Ever? Will you bring her back home to me?'

Thomas jingled the coins in his pockets. 'How much do you think it costs to get to Europe and back, Mother? More than a bag of coconuts? More than one of those humpbacked cows? Where do you think this money comes from?'

'I don't know, I don't know. Don't ask me such things. Maybe it's better for her to stay here, after all. I'm not well. She helps me to carry water. She helps me grow my beans. She's a good child.'

'I want to stay here,' Abela said. She clutched her grandmother's hand tightly. 'I won't go, Bibi. Not without you. I want to look after you.'

'Get her ready,' Thomas ordered. 'I'll fetch her at six.' He strode off to the field that belonged to his mother, and stood with his arms folded, watching the rippling stalks of corn. After a while his mother joined him.

'Abela is ready for you,' she said quietly. 'But I want to know some things. And for a change, you can tell me the truth, Thomas. I've been thinking. How come you managed to marry Susie so quickly, and how come you got all these papers you talked about for Abela, and all in such a rush? Is it something to do with why you got sent away from England? You in trouble there? You in police trouble?'

He laughed. 'Ma, what you don't know, you don't need to know. It's nothing to do with you, old woman.'

'Everything's to do with me. I'm your mother. I know something's wrong here.' She clicked her tongue. 'But just tell me this, then. Where did you get all the money for these papers you needed?'

He shrugged. 'Can't you guess?'

'Tell me. True words. Tell me.'

Her son squatted down on his knees and scooped up a handful of dry earth. He let it trickle between his fingers. Then he looked up at her. Slowly understanding spread across her face.

'My land! You paid for it with my land?'

'*My* land, Ma, when you're dead. Which you soon will be, by the look of you.'

'It belongs to our tribe. You have no right to part with it like this.' His mother's voice screeched with shock and anger. 'Who are these men you gave it to? One tribe will fight another for this land, you know that! It's ours. You have no right to give it away, for any reason.'

He stood up, scattering the last of the dust over her head. 'It's done, Mama. And you better get off it right now. It's not yours any more, not even the corn or the beans that grow on it, not even the dust in your hair.' He clapped his hands at her, shooing her off the field like a straying hen.

'And I'm poor for the rest of my life!' she wailed. She turned on him, beating him with her fists till he gripped her wrists tightly above her head. 'How am I going to live, Thomas?'

'Abela will send you money.'

'Abela?'

'I told you. A rich family will buy her. I give half the money to you, Mama. And Susie is my wife now – she can come and go as she pleases, and when I get to England, I can help her. We'll find more little girls to take to England, more and more. There's no end of rich homes for them. I'm a good son. I'll give you a share. Soon you'll be able to buy your land back. Now what do you think of my plan? Mama, I'm your clever son, not your bad son. I'm good and kind to my old mother.'

After all, there wasn't much more to be done to get Abela ready. Her grandmother had taken some precious last dried beans and eggs down to the market and when she had sold them, she bought Abela another kanga, blue like the sky of Africa. It had a frieze of letters stamped round it. *Utanikumbuka.* You will remember me. One of Bibi's friends gave Abela some old sandals to wear; they were too big, and her feet slipped about inside the loose straps.

'You'll need them,' she told Abela. 'Everybody wears them in Europe.'

They had been a present, posted from Amsterdam many years ago by a tourist who had befriended her. Abela's feet slopped from side to side in them as she ran to the schoolhouse to say goodbye to Mrs Long.

'So you're really going.' Mrs Long shook her head sadly. 'I wish you weren't, Abela. I hope things will be all right for you there. My word, you'll be cold in

England!' She pretended to shiver, pretended to laugh. 'What clothes are you taking?'

'My kangas and my new shoes,' Abela told her, with a touch of pride in her voice.

'Here. You'd better have something warm.' Mrs Long went into her bedroom and came out with a red cardigan. She slipped it round Abela's shoulders and smiled. 'It's huge on you, but the colour suits you.'

'Thank you for my something warm,' Abela said, hugging it round herself even though it made her feel sticky with its heat. 'And thank you for my English words.'

'I'll miss you, Abela. Never forget how beautiful this country is.'

'Yes, Teacha. One day I come home. One day I be doctor, I come home, and I make people better.' She puffed out her cheeks and giggled. It had been a huge sentence for her to say.

The next morning the whole village turned out to say goodbye to Abela.

'*Kwa heri*, *kwa heri*, Abela,' they called to her, laughing excitedly. 'Goodbye, Abela.'

She clutched her new kangas and her Coca-Cola car and the mirror key-ring rolled up in the red cardigan; she had nothing else to take.

'Be a good girl,' Bibi said to her. Her voice was breaking into little pieces.

Suddenly Abela realised the enormity of what was happening. She clung to Bibi, clasping her hands together

110

tight round the old woman's waist, and had to be pulled away roughly by Uncle Thomas as the bus engine revved for departure.

'Tell you something, Abela,' he said quietly. 'Take a long last look. This is the last time we'll be here. Ever.'

He pushed her up the step and she scrambled to a seat by the window, desperate to wave goodbye to her grandmother, to her friends, to all the villagers, to Mrs Long, to the priest who was at that very moment parking his motorbike outside the school; all waved, all smiled, all became ghosts in the shimmer of yellow dust.

On the first part of the journey, Uncle Thomas amused himself by testing her English. She had to repeat after him, 'This is my mother. My father will come home soon.' It didn't make any sense to her but she said it to please him, and when at last he tired of it and put on headphones to listen to sizzly music, she was glad. She didn't want to talk. She didn't really want to think. She gazed blankly out of the window at the figures standing along the road, the occasional flashes of little villages, the mile after mile of emptiness. At last, she fell asleep.

From the time she woke up again, everything was a confusion of bright lights and bustling people, shouting voices, cars and shops, the busy whirl of a big city. Abela had never seen anything like it. It was frightening and exciting; she wanted to stop and wonder at it, the glitter and clamour of it. A beggar with leather pads tied to his knee stumps scooted along on arm crutches; Abela stopped to stare and was pulled away by her uncle. At last they arrived at the airport. She slopped clumsily and tiredly in her loose sandals after her uncle as he hurried her into the frantic airport building.

'Is this Europe?' she asked, and was ignored.

Her uncle was tense and tired after two days of travelling to Korogwe and back, and a heavy night's drinking at the pombe bar in between. She could tell that at least. What she couldn't tell was that he was desperately anxious in case the officials realised there was something wrong with her forged passport and she wasn't allowed on the plane. If he was accused of possessing false documents he would lose his chance for ever of returning to England, but he told her nothing of that. He didn't even know whether she would be allowed to travel on her own. He fished in his rucksack and brought out a loose headscarf, which he draped around Abela's head, covering most of her face. It made her feel hot and sweaty. She tried to pull it off but he slapped her wrist.

'Keep it on till you see Susie,' he ordered her. 'It might help.' He brought out a pair of loose cotton trousers and told her to step into them. Then he stood back. 'That's better,' he said. 'Now you can be anybody.'

He hurried to catch up with two African-Asian women who were joining the queue at the check-in desk. His shirt was dark with sweat. Abela swayed beside him, half-asleep, clinging onto her red bundle.

One of the women in the queue offered her a banana and she took it in grateful silence. Now she could hear her uncle shouting at the man at the desk, arguing in his bullying voice, but she was too tired to try to understand what was going on. He turned his head and gestured towards the women, and the man at the desk nodded and shrugged.

At last it seemed to be over. Uncle Thomas turned round and lifted her up. His face was bright with smiles again. 'She's happy because she's going to see her mother,' he told the women with the bananas, and they smiled at Abela and told her she would be glad of her red cardigan in England. Abela's eyes swam with tears, stinging, tired, uncomprehending tears. How could she be going to see her mother? Her mother was dead.

'The steward at the desk wants to know there is someone to look after her on the flight,' Uncle Thomas told the women.

'All that way on her own!' the older of the two said. 'It's a long, long way!'

'My daughter has to travel on her own. Her mother will meet her at Heathrow. I'm coming next week.'

'I'll look after her,' one of the woman nodded. She smiled at Abela. 'Hey, you don't need to cry. You scared of flying? It's fun!'

When the women went forward to the desk to have their documents checked, Uncle Thomas knelt down to Abela and thrust an envelope and a little book into her hand. 'This is your passport,' he told her. 'Never let anyone else have it, right? Cling hold of it all the time. It cost me a lot of money.'

So this was the passport, this was what all the fuss was about. She opened it curiously and looked at the shiny picture inside. A little girl stared solemnly out at her.

'That's you,' Uncle Thomas said.

She started. 'Me? What do you mean, me?'

'That's your picture. Your photograph.'

She frowned at it, trying to understand. She knew the word *picture*. She stroked the face gently. Did she really look like that?

'What is this?' she asked, holding out the letter.

'That's your HIV certificate. You're to give that to Susie. She'll look after it for you.'

He wiped the sweat away from his face with the back of his hand. 'You'd better put them in something.' He led her to a bookstall and asked for a carrier bag, and all her belongings, her new kanga, her red cardigan, her passport, her Coca-Cola car, her mirror key-ring with the dangling beads, her certificate, went into it. She wrapped the handle tightly round her wrist, proud to have something to carry like everyone else.

Her uncle made a strange gesture to the two women, putting his fist up to his ear. 'I'm just going to phone her mother,' he said, and took Abela to a bank of phones. He whistled impatiently between his teeth while he waited for the number to connect, then snapped some quick and indistinct words into the phone before handing it down to Abela.

'She's there,' he said. 'Speak.'

Abela stared at him and then at the phone. She had never spoken into one of these things before.

'Say hello. Say "Hello, Mummy".'

She jumped when she heard the tinny sound like a strangled voice coming from the phone. She couldn't speak. It would be like talking to Mrs Long's radio.

Uncle Thomas lifted the receiver back to his own ear, laughing, and spoke quick English words into it. Soon his voice was rising, he was shouting again, arguing all to himself. Angrily he slammed the receiver back down.

'She'll be there when you arrive,' he told Abela. 'Your mummy. Susie. Remember to call her Mummy. Always. She's Mummy, and I'm Daddy, not Uncle Thomas any more.' His voice was rough, like a dog's, Abela thought. Like a dog that could bite at any minute. 'It's very, very important. There could be serious trouble with the police if you get it wrong. I could go to prison. Understand?'

She nodded, but she didn't understand, not a word of it, even though it was spoken very carefully in her own language. She was frightened by the tone of his voice.

'Come on, we've got to get you into the departure lounge.' He took her hand and led her to where the two Tanzanian women were waiting for her by the departure gate, and there he squatted down, full of smiles again.

'Give Daddy a big kiss,' he said. His hand was hurting her. She let him hug her, turning her face away from him. 'I'll be with you and Mummy as soon as I can.'

And he walked away quickly, without a backward glance.

I don't remember much about flying to England. It was night when we boarded the plane. It was like getting on a big bus, but I think there were more people on that plane than there are in my village. The two women sat next to me and told me I could have the seat near the window. I didn't think that was a good idea, because it was dark outside anyway, but they just smiled and told me to wait and see. When the plane was setting off I thought it would break up into little pieces; it roared like a herd of charging animals, it rushed like a mighty wind, like the *haboub* of the desert. And then the women told me we were in the air, flying like a huge quiet bird through the night sky; like a massive eagle with people in its belly. I couldn't believe it; even though I had seen these big silver birds in the sky that people called planes, I couldn't believe that I was inside one.

'Look now,' one of the women said. She was fat and comfortable and she reminded me a little of Bibi's neighbour. I liked her best.

Out of the window, far below me, I could see millions of golden and silver lights. 'The plane-bird's flying over the stars!' I gasped, and she laughed and told me that those lights weren't stars at all, but the cars and house lights and streetlamps of the great town of Dar es Salaam. They were beautiful, like strings of glowing beads. And then the lights were fewer and fewer. We were flying over Tanzania, over the plains and mountains and deserts. I thought about Bibi sitting alone outside her little round mud hut, with all the darkness of the night around her. Oh, Bibi!

We were flying over Africa, and still I stared out at the huge black empty night. We left Africa behind. Black, black, black, all around the plane-bird. Black.

I woke up hours later, stiff and hungry. The sky was light, and below us were strange deserts curling and cresting and billowing into wonderful shapes, white and golden and pink, and I was told that they weren't deserts but clouds, and the colours were the light of the sun.

I slept again, and I was woken by that terrible charging rush of the herd of animals. It was the plane landing, bumping down the clouds like a bus bumping over rutted roads, and then it was still.

'We've landed!' the Tanzanian ladies said. 'You're home!'

'Are we in Europe?' I asked.

'We're at Heathrow Airport, London, England,' the plump one said.

'Europe,' added the tall one with the smiling eyes.

'Heathrow Airport, London, England, Europe,' I repeated, and kept on repeating it while we went through the terminal and waited for their baggage, and all the way through into the arrivals lounge; I held onto it like a chant, because it was a magical song. My village had gone. Tanzania had gone. Africa had gone. Heathrow,

London, England, Europe had been put in its place. This was where I lived now.

I looked for Susie among all the white women at the airport. The faces all looked the same, and most of them had yellow hair. White faces, yellow hair, tiny mouths.

'She's not here,' I told them.

'Then we'll wait,' the plump one said comfortably, and they sat with me as if they had all the time in the world, as if they were just sitting in the Tanzanian sunshine waiting for a bus that might be one, five, ten hours late, it didn't matter. They would wait for days, if they had to. They would wait for Susie.

And at last I saw her, my white princess, my flamingo. She didn't see me; in fact, she walked right past me. I grabbed out at the sleeve of her jacket. And I remembered the right word.

'Mummy!'

She snapped round, frowning, and I remembered then to pull the hot scarf away from my head.

'There you are!'

I put my arms round her waist and hugged her. I could smell flowery perfume on her jacket.

'I thought you weren't coming!' I sobbed in my own language. I couldn't find any English words to tell her how frightened and lonely I felt. *Be a good girl*, my grandmother's voice said to me. *Be strong*, my mother said, in her pretty blue voice. *Be strong, be strong, and be strong*.

'Ah, Mummy's come now! Now you're a happy girl!' The two Tanzanian women picked up their bags and strolled away into their lives, leaving me alone with Susie.

'Why did you call me Mummy?' she asked. Her voice was jagged and red; it hurt the air. I didn't like it.

I faltered. I could sense that something was wrong. 'He say me to. Daddy say me.' I leaned closer to her and whispered. 'You know, Uncle Thomas.'

'I see.' She straightened up, smiling. 'Well, I think I know what I can do now. Clever Daddy.'

I lived with Susie for two months. At first we stayed in a room with a big bed and a box that held all Susie's clothes. The room was as big as Bibi's house, but Susie said it was a dive, which meant it was too small and dark and nasty, and she was ashamed to be living there. 'I can't afford anything better. I spent all my money on going to Africa with Thomas,' she told me. 'And he has every penny that was left. Every damn cent.' She lit a cigarette and dragged on it, making her cheeks hollow and ugly. 'But I'll get us out of here. You'll see.'

One day she wrapped me up in one of her jackets; the sleeves were so long that she had to roll them up, but at least I was warm and snug in it. I loved it because it smelt of her perfume. She took me along to a place called Housing Department. She told me to say nothing at all, and I didn't, but I listened to every word, trying to piece the few familiar words together to make some

119

kind of sense, but she spoke too fast, jabber jabber jabber, and all I caught were the words daughter, husband, Africa. Oh, and home. She argued for a long time, while I tried to understand the words that were flying backwards and forwards between them. I hated her angry voice; it made me think of the day she had turned against me at Bibi's house, the day I called the HIV/Aids day. Then she stood up and walked out, holding my hand tightly. When we were outside she bent down and hugged me, her face bright with a beautiful smile again.

'They've given me a family flat!' she told me, laughing, and I laughed too. I wanted her to be happy like this all the time. 'There'll be a bed for me and a bed for you, a little room with a table to cook our meals, and a bathroom for us to wash in, all to ourselves. And we can have it straight away! All because of you, Abela!'

The next day we put all her clothes into carrier bags and walked to the new flat. Susie was ecstatic. She picked me up under the armpits and whirled me round. 'Look, look, enough room to swing a child in!' she laughed. 'And I'd never have got this if it wasn't for you. You have to have a child to be given a flat like this, and now I've got one! And soon I'll have a husband here too, and we'll all live together and be very, very happy.'

How I loved it when Susie was happy! She read me stories and made me a book with drawings of animals, and we wrote the names in English and Swahili. *Simba,* lion. *Twiga*, giraffe. *Kuku*, chicken. She drew the pictures and gave me some pencils to colour them in with. On the back page she sellotaped a piece of paper.

'What's that?' I asked.

'It's the paper that Thomas gave you in that envelope,' she said. 'Keep it safe, Abela. It tells people that you don't have Aids, thank God.'

Sometimes she went out to work at a café nearby, and left me to get on with my colouring.

'Can I come with you?' I asked her, but she always refused.

'No. It isn't safe.'

'I want to go out. Can I go to school?'

She shook her head.

'When Thomas comes. He said I must keep you at home till he comes. Anyway, you don't need to go to school,' she said. 'I can teach you.' She switched on the television set, the magic box that somebody in one of the other flats had given her. 'Watch that. You'll learn everything you need to know.'

I don't think she ever switched it off after that. It chattered and screeched all day, coloured lights like eyes blinking, flash, flash, flash, jangly music, voices, words words words, day and night.

One day she brought me some clothes that someone had given her, and we spent hours sorting through them, cutting them and sewing them so I had a dress and a skirt that fitted me. In those days she was always happy, and I was happy too. She said I made her life better.

And she made my life better. Every time she came home to the empty, flashing chattering flat she brought smiles and hugs and the sharp, cold smell of England with her. Her carrier bag was always full of food from the café – bags of lukewarm chips, soggy apple pie. We ate together in front of the television and she told me funny stories about the customers.

But things changed. Something was wrong, but I didn't know what. Thomas was supposed to be ringing her every week and she would go out to the phone box on the corner. She wouldn't take me with her. I would sit on the windowsill watching her, waiting for her to come back, and when she did she would be looking white and miserable; she would go to her room and shut the door and stay there for hours. She grew tired of me, and there was nothing I could do to please her. I tried everything I could think of to make her smile at me. I cooked all her meals, I cleaned the flat, I washed her clothes, and the more I did, the more she seemed to hate me. Sometimes I thought she couldn't bear the sight of me. She went out to work more often, sometimes she stayed out all night, and when she came back she was tired and grumpy. She would tell me to leave her alone.

'Why doesn't he come!' she shrieked at me once in that red, jagged voice that frightened me. 'He's no intention of coming, has he? You've tricked me, all of you. What do I want with a kid of your age? I've got my own life to lead. Why should I have a kid like you tagging round me?'

But the worst thing was the fact that she wouldn't let me go out. In all that time, two or three months or more, I only went outside twice, once to the Housing Department and once when we moved from one flat to another. I used to sit by the window in my room and look outside at the grey streets and the cars and the restless people. I saw children playing, and wished I could be with them. Even when it rained, I wished I could be outside. But in my country the rain is alive. The rain sings with life. Here it is a grey mist that closes up the world.

One day when she came back from the phone box she was in a different kind of mood. I heard the front door slamming when she came in, I heard her footsteps ringing round the stairwell as she stamped up the concrete stairs. She flung open the door to the flat and glared down at me. I was truly afraid. She grabbed me with both hands and shook my shoulders.

'Still not coming!' she shouted. 'What kind of a marriage is this? Eh? You knew all along, you brat!' She knelt down, hissing in my ear. 'He wants me to sell you to a rich family so he can buy his way over. What would happen to you then, eh? You can thank your stars he isn't coming yet, because that's where you'd be now, Cinderella in the cellar, that's who you'd be. Heard of Cinderella?'

I shook my head, numb with fright at this new passion of anger.

'Heard of slaves, then? Think it was all over hundreds of years ago? No way, kiddo. No way.'

I still had no idea what she was talking about. Being sold to a rich family didn't sound such a bad idea to me.

'So till he comes and finds somewhere for me, you can be *my* slave! Why not? Pay for your keep for a change.'

My eyes were filling up with tears. What more could I do for her? Every day I washed Susie's clothes and put them away nice and tidy. I cooked her lovely food and washed up the dishes and kept the flat clean and sweet.

'There's plenty for you to do,' Susie snapped at me. 'I've got myself another job at the café – they've asked me to do a bit of washing for them – tablecloths and tea towels and that. No way, I said. I'm a waitress, me! But you could do that, Bella. And if you don't do it right, I've got a big slap on the end of my arm. Do it right and we'll be friends. Do it wrong and I'll sell you on to someone else. And that would be like sending you to Hell. Heard of Hell, have you?'

'Will I go to the café, then?' I asked. That wouldn't be too bad. I would smell the fresh air, I would run, run and feel free.

Susie put her face close to mine. I could smell the sharp, nasty tang of her cigarettes on her breath, and I tried to back away, but she gripped me by the shoulders. Her fingers were like the talons of big birds, like the vultures.

'Come to the café?' she laughed, but it wasn't the white-moon laugh that she used to have. 'You've got to be joking. You're not moving from this place till

Thomas gets here and sells you on, so you can forget that. You stay here, right here, or you'll go to a much worse place. And don't go peering out of that window either. You've no time for that. Soon as I get the stuff from work, you can get busy. And you can start now.' She marched me into her room and pulled out a pile of dirty underclothes from under her bed. 'Here you are. Get working on that lot.'

Abela could never judge Susie's moods after that. Sometimes she was bewitchingly happy. She would put a CD on and swirl round the flat in her creamy silky nightclothes, a cigarette in one hand with a blush of lipstick on the stub. She would grab Abela by the other hand and make her dance with her, round and round, heads flung back, till they were both laughing and dizzy. Sometimes she would scoop Abela up in her arms and shower her with kisses, and tell her that Uncle Thomas was coming soon, very soon, and she wouldn't let him sell her, she loved Abela too much. They would all live as one happy family.

And at other times she was deep in a black mood, sultry and dark as a cloud of thunder. She wouldn't speak, wouldn't eat the food Abela cooked for her, would sit in front of the television in a deep blue fog of cigarette smoke. At these times Abela would creep quietly about her work, washing the pieces of laundry that Susie brought from the café, hanging them over the radiators to dry, ironing them smooth and crisp, till her back ached and her arms hurt and she longed to lie down and sleep. Maybe life is all like this in England, she thought. Maybe this is what all the children have to do. But then from time to time she would hear the high voices of children running to school or playing in the street outside. Only when Susie was out would she dare to steal a glimpse of them from the window.

We never had visitors, ever. Susie had no friends. When I was with my mother and father I was outside all day, helping my father with the animals, helping my mother with the maize, playing with my cousins. Outside was where we lived. There were no walls to the church or the schoolhouse; we only went into the house to sleep. People drifted from one hut to another, '*Hodi, hodi*,' they would call, picking their feet over the chickens, and they would come and sit round the cooking pots and talk and talk. Oh, Bibi!

Then one day there was a knock at the door of the flat. We both thought immediately that it must be Thomas. I was in my room, ironing aprons with the door open, so I could watch the flickering television screen. I saw Susie patting her hair into place before she ran to the door and pulled it open. But it wasn't Thomas, of course it wasn't. A lady in a very wet blue coat and hair like white feathers showed Susie her identity card and said she was from social services. Susie tried to close the door in her face, but the lady stepped forward and said she needed to see me, and Susie came into my room and pulled me out, slamming my door behind me. She dug her fingers into my arm, just like Uncle Thomas used to do.

'Keep your mouth shut!' she warned me, hissing in my ear like a fat snake.

The woman sat down and smiled at me. Wet drips trickled down her coat onto the floor. She asked me how old I was, but I was too frightened to tell her.

'She's not very big. You're about seven, I would think.'

I knew that was wrong but I daren't say anything.

'We're concerned because you haven't registered your daughter for school here yet,' the woman said to Susie.

School! I heard the word and nursed it like a present. How I wanted to go to school!

Susie sat down slowly at the table. I could see that her hand was shaking. She had a red flush across her neck.

'She doesn't speak English well enough.'

The woman frowned. 'Why doesn't she speak English? Don't you talk to her in English?'

'She's spent all her life in Tanzania. She's been living with her father and her grandmother. Now she's come home.' Susie looked at me and smiled, a smile that was as cold as the window feels when the rain is beating against the other side, and the smile said, *Keep quiet*. And I did keep quiet.

'We have been told that you go out to work,' the woman said. 'Is this true?'

'Sometimes,' Susie said. Her voice was shaking. 'Just a bit, now and then.'

'And do you take your daughter with you?'

'Oh yes.'

The woman asked me some questions, and I was too frightened to hear what she said, never mind to answer her. But my head was spinning.

'She must come to school,' the woman said. 'It's against the law to keep a child away from school, you must know that. She'll soon learn English there.'

I wanted to shout then that I could speak English, that Mrs Long said I was the best pupil she had ever taught and that I was clever enough to be a doctor one day: that I wanted, wanted, wanted to go to school. But I stared at the little puddle on the floor and kept quiet.

As soon as the woman went, I asked Susie why I couldn't go to school.

'Because you can't!' she snapped. *Can't* hung in the air like a piece of old rag in the wind. 'Not till Thomas comes. I've told you! I can't register you anywhere. We need more papers! Birth certificate, things like that! Why doesn't he send them? Why the hell doesn't he come? Oh, he's got me in such a mess. It's not your fault. It's him. I don't want to be mixed up in his game.' She ran her fingers through her hair, and I realised then how limp and ragged it looked these days, not at all golden and glowing like it used to be. Her face was thin and she had dark caves round her eyes. For a moment she softened; for a moment she put her arms round me and held me tight. 'I don't know what to do!' she said, in a wailing voice like a little girl, but when I lifted my arms up round her waist to comfort her, she pushed me away.

'Why did you have to come!' she hissed. 'Everything's gone wrong! I don't want you here!'

I longed for home. I spent hours in my little room, gazing out of the window at the forbidden street outside. I longed to be running barefoot from my grandmother's house to my school, or playing in the sand with my friends, or singing in the church with the birds swooping in and out and right through because they thought it belonged to them. Bibi, Bibi, I used to whisper, so my breath made a little cloud on the glass. And sometimes in the night I would hear Susie whisper, 'Thomas, Thomas.' I knew then that we were whispering about the same thing. I would never see Bibi again, I knew that now. And Susie knew that she would never see Thomas.

The lady came back, several times, but Susie didn't answer the door. She called through the door to us, and Susie kept her fingers pressed into my arm, so they hurt. Her long talon nails cut little circles into my flesh. When the woman went, silence swirled round the flat like a cold mist.

'Perhaps I should go to school,' I said at last.

'Oh go then, go!' she snapped. 'Go to Timbuktu, for all I care!'

But she didn't take me to school, and I had no idea where to go. So, one day, I decided to just find it. I could go to school and still do my work at night, I decided.

Susie wouldn't mind, when she saw how hard I would work and how happy I would be. I would find the school, no matter where it was. After all, at home I could walk for hours, days, to find a place I had never been to before. I took my chance on the morning she stayed in bed instead of going out to work. She said she had a headache, and didn't want to eat the breakfast I made for her. There was the key, on the table next to her bed. There was my freedom. I put her cup of tea down and slid my fingers round the key.

'Go away,' she groaned. 'Just leave me alone.'

My time had come to be strong. I decided not to wear the clothes that Susie had made for me, but to wear the clothes from home, so I would feel proud and brave. I put on my favourite kanga that was as blue as the sky of Africa, and Mrs Long's cardigan, and the shoes that Bibi's friend had given to me. I let myself out of the flat with the key, and I tiptoed down the echoey concrete stairs. My heart throbbed like a drum in my chest. But I couldn't open the door downstairs, the key didn't fit the lock. I pushed and pulled the handle, but nothing happened. I wanted to scream with frustration. I couldn't bear the thought of going back upstairs again, now that I had set my heart on going to school. I sat on the floor, pounding my fists against the door, and at last the woman from the downstairs flat opened her door and glared at me. Her belly was big and round.

'What's all this noise about?' she asked.

'I want go school,' I said. 'Please open door.'

'Ah! School!' she grunted. 'About time too.'

She unlocked the door, and I stepped into the sharp March morning.

It was bitterly cold. The sharp wind knifed between the blocks of flats. White flakes drifted on it. Abela thought they were flakes of ash from a fire somewhere, but when they settled on her they melted and gleamed into drops of rain. She looked up at the fluttering sleet and thought the grey sky was breaking into tiny pieces all round her. She had never been so cold in her life, but she began to run, swinging her arms backwards and forwards across her chest, her loose sandals slapping the pavement. She ran to the end of the street where she had watched children walking with their mothers, and down another, and swung into another. From somewhere nearby she could hear the high, excited voices of children playing; the dream sound. She darted over a road, right in the path of a car that screamed to a halt, and she skipped away from it and down another street, and there, at the end, was a yard full of children. She found a gate and ran into the yard, clasping her hands to her mouth in sheer joy, her face so full of smiling that it ached.

The children were just beginning to file into the school building. Abela followed them in. Some of them turned their heads to stare at her, and exchanged smiling looks at the strange way she was dressed on such a cold morning, but apart from that nobody seemed to take much notice of her. The children made their way to a large hall and sat

131

cross-legged on the floor, and so did she. Now she was noticed. A man wearing a brown woolly jumper leaned forward and tried to catch her attention, but then, another man walked up to the front of the hall and turned to face them all, and the hall went completely silent.

'Good morning, children,' the new man, the school head teacher, said.

A chorus of children's voices rumbled, 'Good morning, Mister Helliwell. Good morning, everybody.'

'Good mornin', Teacha!' Abela called out, and some of the children in the row in front of her turned round to stare. She grinned back at them. The head teacher talked on and on, and Abela gazed round the hall at the bright pictures on the walls, the high windows with their long, colourful curtains, the shiny black piano, the line of teachers sitting on chairs along the side of the room. The man with the brown woolly jumper was staring intently at her again. He was nice, she thought. She smiled at him, and he wiggled one of his fingers at her. She didn't know it was a signal for her to go to him, so she lifted her hand and did the same, then laughed and covered her face, rocking herself backwards and forwards out of sheer happiness.

There was a sudden scuffling sound, and she realised that the head teacher had stopped talking and all the children were standing and turning to face her.

'*Jambo!*' she said.

The children immediately facing her giggled.

'Turn round!' one of the girls whispered. 'Go to class!'

But the teacher in the woolly jumper had moved forward now. He told his children to go to class and sit quietly and wait for him, then he touched Abela's arm lightly and led her away from them. He stopped near the head teacher, folded his arms and smiled at Abela. She smiled back.

'Now then. Who are you?' he asked, too quickly for her to understand.

She frowned. 'Mornin', Teacha,' she tried.

'OK. I'll try again. What is your name?'

'Oh. My name is Abela.'

'Bella?'

'I am called Abela Mbisi. How are you?' Mrs Long had taught her to say that. Far, far away, in another life.

'Hello, Abela,' he said slowly. 'My name is Mister Hardy. Come and meet Mister Helliwell.'

He took her over to where the headmaster was telling a boy off for eating his lunch during assembly.

'I wasn't!' protested the boy, wiping cheese crumbs off his sweatshirt.

'This is Abela Mbisi,' Mister Hardy said. 'And I've never seen her before. Is she one of ours?'

'Bella Mbisi,' the head teacher repeated. 'No, I don't know that name. Come with me, Bella, and we'll sort you out.'

'Abela, her name is. I'll see to my class,' said Mister Hardy.

Abela's smile faded. This wasn't right. She wanted to go with the man in the woolly jumper. She turned to watch him as he made his way down the hall. The boy with the empty lunchbox punched the air and slid away, joyfully forgotten.

'Come on, Bella.'

She followed Mister Helliwell. She was frightened in case he was going to take her back to Susie's flat and leave her there, but instead he led her into a room that was full of books and papers, photographs of groups of beaming children, and gleaming trophies. A woman sitting at a desk near the window looked up and smiled at her.

'Hello!' she said. 'What a lovely dress.'

Mister Helliwell sat down on a green leather chair that swivelled from one side to another, and pulled some papers towards him. He looked at Abela thoughtfully, then took a pen from a jar and clicked down the nib. He handed the pen to Abela.

'Can you write your name?' he asked.

She wrote slowly and carefully, anxious to show him how good her handwriting was.

'Ah. *Abela*. I see. Now, Abela, where do you live?'

She frowned. She had no idea.

'Do you understand?'

'Yes, Teacha.' She brightened up, remembering her chant. 'Heathrow Airport, London, England, Europe.'

Both Mister Helliwell and his secretary smiled. 'OK. That's very good. And where do you sleep?' he asked.

'In my bed.' She was very pleased with her English. She thought that must be why he was smiling.

'Where's your mother?' the secretary tried.

'Mama is dead.'

Mister Helliwell bowed his head for a moment. 'Your father?'

'Baba is dead.'

'I see. And who brought you here this morning, Abela? Do you understand? Who looks after you? Where do you live? Who do you live with?'

Oh dear. So many questions. All Abela wanted was to show him how good she was at English so he would let her stay in school. 'I live in Africa,' she said slowly. 'But now I live in Susie house.'

'Where is it, Abela? What's the address?'

She didn't know that word, address. She closed her eyes, trying to picture the flat and the view from the window. Where was it? It was in a street. 'Social service house,' she said at last.

'Good girl,' said the secretary. 'That's a big help. I'll see what I can find out.'

'Could you take me there?' Mister Helliwell asked.

She drew away, biting her lip. The thought of being taken back to the flat was more than she could bear, to be locked up again day after day, week after week, till Uncle Thomas came. 'Please, Teacha, don't take me back. I want stay here.' There was something like a hard stone in her throat, so hard that she couldn't swallow. She could hardly speak. There was more to say, she knew that, before the stone could be dislodged. But if she said what she wanted to say, it might bring terrible

135

trouble. She put her hands over her face, and Mister Helliwell's secretary came and knelt by her and put her arm across her shoulders.

'It's all right, Abela,' she whispered. 'You can tell us everything.'

Abela took a deep breath. 'Susie not Mummy,' she whispered back. 'She pretend so we get social service flat.' The secretary nodded, encouraging her to say more. 'She say me I not come to school. No papers, no birth tifick.'

'No birth certificate. I see. What about a passport?'

'Susie tell me it pretend passport, it bring very bad trouble.'

There, it was out. She saw the slow look that Mister Helliwell exchanged with his secretary. She heard his deep, deep sigh.

'Illegal immigrant,' the secretary said.

'Looks like it. Looks very like it,' Mister Helliwell agreed. 'Oh dear.'

Abela lifted her head, deeply scared now. She had one last chance, she felt, before he sent her to prison. 'But I want come to school. I want be clever doctor. All people sick, all people dying, like Mama, like Baba. Like my baby sister.' Now the tears were pricking her eyes, but she forced them back. *Be strong, be strong, my little kuku.*

'Look, Abela, I'll tell you what we'll do,' Mister Helliwell said. 'You can stay in Mister Hardy's class this morning while I sort out what to do with you.'

Abela nodded. She didn't understand everything he

said, but he wasn't angry with her, that was the main thing. It wasn't so important, after all, not to have the right papers. Susie was mistaken. Maybe she would be happy now, when she found out.

Mister Helliwell led her to one of the classrooms and tapped on the door. She twisted the corner of her kanga into a tight knot in her fist when he pushed open the door and all the children turned round to stare at her.

'I think Abela would like to make a nice friend here,' he said.

Mister Hardy smiled at her. 'Welcome, Abela,' he said. 'How about sitting next to Jasmine?'

A girl with olive skin and gleaming black hair patted the empty seat next to her, and there she sat, quiet and wide-eyed, watching Mister Hardy as he walked about the room, soaking up the atmosphere of the classroom, and whenever anyone looked at her she smiled for utter glee. She was in school at last.

At lunchtime she joined the jostling queue in the school hall with Jasmine for something called cheesy squares and cabbage, served on a yellow plastic plate. She chose a banana as well, because she hadn't seen one since she left home. She and Jasmine ate side by side, saying nothing, giggling from time to time. She felt perfectly happy, until somebody came and told her to go to Mister Helliwell's office. Her happiness drained away from her. So, she thought, he has found out what to do with me. Maybe he will whip me now because I have no papers.

As she stood outside the office she could hear a familiar voice, and she shrank back, trying to remember where she had heard the voice before. She associated it with Susie's red anger moods, and it frightened her. She turned to run away, but Mister Helliwell came to the door and nodded to her to come in. There was a white-haired stranger sitting there, and Abela recognised her at once as the woman who had come to Susie's flat and told her that Abela should be at school.

She smiled when she saw Abela, and held out her hand to her. 'So, Abela, you found your way to school after all. I'm very pleased. Do you like it?'

Abela nodded. 'Please no go home.'

'Don't worry. You can stay here today, and you can come back tomorrow.'

Abela relaxed. The woman stood up and came towards her, then bent down to be close to her. Abela could smell fried tomatoes on her breath.

'Actually, you can't go home tonight, Abela. Not to the flat.'

Abela tried to make sense of the words. 'Not Susie house? Where is Susie?'

'I'm afraid Susie has been taken away by the police. She has a lot of questions to answer. Do you understand?'

Abela nodded again, but her mind was blank with terror now. All she really understood was the word *police*. This was what Uncle Thomas had warned her about, in his growling dog voice. What had she done? Was this all her fault, after all? Why had she told Mister

138

Helliwell so much?

The woman with feathery hair smiled at her again, trying to show her that everything would be all right. 'I'm called Mrs Sanderson. I'm here to help you. I'm going to be your social worker while you're in England. Your friend. And I've already found somewhere for you to live, very near here. Someone who will look after you till you go home to Tanzania again. You have a false passport, Abela. You can't stay in this country. We're going to try to find your family so we can send you home again.'

Abela stared at her. There was too much to understand, so she understood nothing. 'Where is Susie?' she asked again. She had the corner of her kanga screwed up in both her hands. Gently, Mrs Sanderson eased her fingers open and smoothed the fabric down again.

'Susie's been evicted from the flat. She can't live there any more. She's with the police at the moment,' Mrs Sanderson said. She sighed and stood up, tucking a green fabric briefcase under her arm. 'You don't understand, do you? She'll be all right, Abela. Don't worry about her.'

'Why don't you go back and play with Jasmine?' Mister Helliwell said, and Abela turned immediately and ran from his office. Words that made no sense to her buzzed like flies in her head. All she knew was that Susie was in trouble, and that it must be her fault. And was there something about Tanzania? Was she going back tonight? And what about Uncle Thomas? He would be angry, very angry. He would beat her, she was quite sure of that.

Mrs Sanderson stood in the doorway of the head-master's office, watching her. 'Poor child, what a mess. She hasn't a clue what's going on. I must try to find a Swahili speaker to explain all that to her. I'm actually standing in for a colleague who's just back from a long holiday in East Africa. She might be able to help.'

'But why can't she go back to Susie?' the secretary asked. 'She's lost everything, poor child – and now she can't even stay with the woman who's been looking after her. How can you do this to her?'

'It's out of my hands. Susie's in trouble with the police for benefit fraud, claiming single parent benefit when Abela isn't even her child. But, quite apart from anything else, this Susie woman says she doesn't want to have anything more to do with the child,' Mrs Sanderson told her. 'She didn't want her in the first place. It seems that she was trying to get a passport for a man who was an illegal immigrant. It sounds as if he rigged up some kind of false marriage out in Tanzania. Now she realises that he has no hope of coming back to England, she wants nothing more to do with him or his niece. And quite frankly, that's the best thing that could happen for Abela. Susie's been using her like a little servant, according to the woman in the flat below. She's kept her locked up in the flat for weeks.'

'So what will happen to Abela? Maybe I could help the child.' The secretary was rapidly doing calculations in her head. If she put one daughter in her son's room, maybe they could just squeeze Abela into their house . . . No, how could they get another bed in that room? She shook her head. It wouldn't work.

'I've been authorised to find a temporary place of safety for her, so she'll be properly looked after in a foster home while she's in this country,' Mrs Sanderson said. 'She'll be all right now. She'll be back home soon with her own family. And meanwhile, we've found just the right place for her to stay.'

12
ROSA

So Molly came back to see us. It was like Christmas all over again, I was so excited. I half expected her to bring my new sister with her, but she came on her own, with forms to fill and lots of questions to ask. She asked me if I was really sure about it this time, and I said, yes, yes, a hundred per cent yes, as soon as possible.

She came again a few days later and met Nana and Grandpa, who said they fully supported Mum and me in our decision to adopt, and that they would help us in every way. Grandpa wasn't the slightest bit curmudgeonly that day, in fact I think the new word for him has to be jovial. He kept rubbing his hands together and saying he couldn't wait for a new little scamp to come along, because I was getting too well-behaved and boring. He borrowed a video camera from one of his Art class friends and made a film of our house, all the rooms and the garden, and Mum and me doing things in the kitchen, so the new sister, as I called her, would be able to know all about us before she came. Mum told me to wear my normal, comfortable clothes, not my sparkly shoes, but I did clip a white flower on the side of each of my school shoes. Twitchy played a star part, mincing her way right up to the lens and purring into it.

If cats could smile, she was beaming. I hope my new sister likes cats.

And then, we just had to wait. It was all I could think about. Every day I expected to come home and find the new sister sitting there grinning at me in the kitchen; even though Mum and Molly both warned me that it could take months to find the right child, I still hoped. I decided she would be with us by Easter. I would make her a chocolate cake with a little yellow chicken on top. I would share my Easter eggs with her.

Then one day when I came out of school, Mum was there waiting for me, shivering and smiling in the cold March wind. She said that Molly had rung her to say that she was coming round later with some news. My heart dropped right into my stomach. We practically ran home, clutching hands. I went straight up to my room and started to unravel the mess in it. I even took the Dyson up and sucked Twitchy hairs off the carpet. Finally, finally, I heard the car, and I shoved the last lot of socks and books and stuff under my bed. I prettied up the pile of softies and ran to the window, peering through the new mermaid-green curtains.

She was on her own. I was desolate.

I heard her and Mum talking in the hall, but I couldn't get myself out of my room somehow; not yet. This is it, I kept thinking. This is the day when my life changes for ever. I was on the verge of never being an only child again. I heard them go into the kitchen and shut the door, and I managed to persuade my feet to take me

143

down the stairs. I sat on the bottom step, hugging my knees, straining to hear something of what they were saying. Nothing, only rumblings and mutterings like our central heating when it's kicking off in the morning. A lot from Molly. Long pauses from Mum. Then long pauses from both of them. My eyes wandered. And I saw a pair of boots by the door. Molly's new boots.

They were beautiful. Disappointingly and definitely, they were the wrong colour for the kind of clothes Molly wears; a kind of donkey brown. I crept across and stroked them. Oh, but they were soft suede like Twitchy's nose, knee-length, the sort that are as fluffy inside as Nana's comfy slippers, and that flop over like sleeping cats when nobody's wearing them, but are as smart as a million dollars' worth when they've got legs inside. They had a deep pattern of white stitching round the top, like Egyptian hieroglyphs, as if they were telling an ancient story. That's what I loved about them. I couldn't take my eyes off them. And without thinking twice about it, I did something stupid. I don't excuse myself except to say that I have a passion for shoes like Grandpa has a passion for the piano. I can't leave them alone.

So that's how my feet found themselves inside Molly's boots. They were a bit tight, so I pressed them down. I ran upstairs to look at them in the long mirror. Definitely the wrong colour. A deep plum, or bluey-green – that should be Molly's colour. But they were gorgeous. I preened myself backwards and forwards, hitching my skirt up over my knee, twirling and twisting to look over my shoulder at myself, and then Mum called me and I panicked. I couldn't get them off. Molly's feet must be a whole size smaller than mine. I sat on the floor and pulled, I lay on my bed and heaved. She called me again, and ran upstairs. Molly ran after her. And there I was, writhing and kicking, and Mum was hauling on one foot, shouting at me, and Molly was tugging on the other foot and making a strange sort of hooting noise, and I thought, I've blown it now. She'll never trust us with a defenceless child.

Later, in the calm of the kitchen, Mum massaged my red feet with peppermint oil. Molly had gone now, snug in her boots and still chuckling. She left an envelope on the table with some photographs in, and I knew exactly what they were. They were photographs of my new sister.

'It's not what you expect,' Mum warned me. 'Molly told me it's hard to find Tanzanian children up for adoption in this country.'

I hardly heard her. I couldn't take my eyes off the envelope, and as soon as Mum let go of my feet I hobbled over to the table and opened the envelope. I spread out the photographs one by one on the table and stared at them.

They were all wrong. The child was about four years old. It was a boy.

13
ABELA

That afternoon, when school was finished, I watched Jasmine running to meet her mother in the yard. At the gate she turned round and pointed to me, and her mother waved. All the children left, climbing into big cars, and I was called back by Mister Helliwell's secretary and told to wait in his office. She gave me a chocolate biscuit. I had never tasted one before, and I loved it. Then the lady with hair like white feathers arrived, full of bustle and smiles, and took me in her car to a strange house.

'This is where you're going to live, till you go back home,' she said. 'Come in and meet your foster mother. Her name is Mrs Oladipo, and she's from Nigeria. She has two big children of her own, and two more foster girls, Cathy and Lola. They're both older than you.'

I kept my fingers screwed up inside my hands. I could not find words to talk, or mouth to smile. I did not like the house. I didn't like the carpet, like bright red grass on the floors. I did not like the big children who gaped and laughed at me there. And I did not like the fat woman who was called my foster mother and who said I must call her Carmel. She did not speak my language. She was loud; she snorted through her nose like a horse. She spat when she talked, shouting at me to make me understand her,

146

shrieking loud laughter when I didn't. I did not like her at all.

And I did not like the man who was called Dad by some children and The Dad by others. He had huge, flat hands which he slapped the table with when he was sitting down, as if he was beating a rhythm on a drum. His face was shiny, his hair and his beard were crozzly white, and his eyes stared at me as if they would make holes right through me. He never smiled, not once, and his voice growled from somewhere deep in his stomach.

Carmel showed me up to the room I was to share with the other girls. I had to climb a ladder to get into my bed, and there I found a plastic carrier bag with my other kanga in it, the dress Susie had made for me before she stopped liking me, the book of animals that we had made together, my Coca-Cola car, my pretty key-ring. My passport had gone. I sat on the bed, clutching my car. Carmel wanted me to go downstairs and eat but I wouldn't. She brought me a plate of bread and jam and shouted at me to climb down off my bed and eat it. She was smiling and laughing in her loud, snorting way, but she still shouted, and I covered my ears with my hands and told her to go away.

'Oh, so you're a naughty little girl,' she said. 'We don't have naughty little girls here. Oh no.'

She took the sandwiches away and closed the door. I lay clutching my book and my car while darkness crept around me. The other children came up, and the big girl sleeping in the bed below bounced up and down to make the whole frame shake, and then pushed my mattress up and down

147

from below to try to make me roll off. I didn't care about her. She was annoying, like the grabbing monkeys at home, but I didn't care. I wanted to know where Susie was. I wanted to know what was going to happen to me.

After a bit Carmel opened the door again with my plate of sandwiches in her hand. The other girls lay as still as snakes. She shook my nightie in front of me, laughing and snorting and spraying into my face. I didn't like her. I didn't want to be in her house. She sent me to the bathroom, and when I came back, the big girls were eating my sandwiches. I lay in the dark, listening to them giggling and whispering, and I tried to close my ears till I was in the church at home with the birds swooping in and out and all the people singing in harmony, and Mama's sweet blue voice rising right up to heaven. But just as I was drifting off to sleep the girl below lifted up the springs under my mattress with her feet, kicking and laughing so I had to cling onto the side of the bed. I wouldn't let myself go to sleep after that. I was frightened that if I did, I would fall into a deep black hole, and I would never be able to climb out again.

I whispered to Susie that I was sorry. *I am sorry. I am sorry.* The other big girl shouted at me to shut up but I kept on and on repeating it. *I am sorry. I am sorry.* If I stopped saying it, if I stopped hearing my own voice, I would disappear for ever into the black hole. The girl got out of bed and climbed up my ladder and started hitting me.

Blue fireflies zizzed in the darkness. Little frogs crickled. Mama sang to me.

14
ROSA

I didn't want Anthony to come. I had set my heart on having a sister, someone nearly my age; a best friend. I could do her hair, I could lend her my clothes. I'd look after her, and share my secrets and my favourite CDs. I didn't want a little boy. But I knew I couldn't let Mum down again. I couldn't change my mind, not this time.

'It's not a girl, Mum,' was all I said. 'Don't you mind?'

'Well, maybe we have to take what comes.' Mum gathered up the photographs like a pack of cards and fanned them out in her hand, selecting one and then another. 'After all, a natural mother can't choose whether she has a boy or a girl. And look at him, Rosa. He's beautiful.'

He was. He had huge melting brown eyes and a smile that was as wide as a letter box. Molly brought us a video of him playing with a puppy in his foster-mother's house and he was like a puppy himself, tumbling and play-scrapping and making happy little yapping noises.

'He looks a real cheerful little chap. It's amazing, after what he's been through,' Mum said for the tenth time, and at last I gave in and asked her to tell me what his story was.

This was it, Anthony's story: he was born in Tanzania. His mother was black, his father was white. His parents came to England and they were involved in a train derailment when he was a baby. His mother died. His father was seriously ill for months. So was baby Anthony, but when he was better he was put in the care of a foster mother. His father took him back when he was out of hospital, but he wasn't really better, he couldn't cope. Then he was ill with depression for months, so Anthony was back with the foster mother. The father married again, the new wife wouldn't have Anthony. She wanted a family of her own. She wanted white children. And so, Anthony was placed for adoption.

I know Anthony's story backwards. It's another fairytale, like mine, another life crammed into a few sentences. If I was a writer I could sit down and write a whole book just about Anthony, just about those four years of his life.

And Mum, just by knowing his story, his *case history* as Molly called it, just by looking at his photographs and watching a video of him tumbling over like a puppy, giggling into the camera, had fallen completely in love with him. She went to see him, and she came back with stars in her eyes, bubbling over with stories about him. He had charmed her socks off. His social worker brought him to see us one Saturday after skating, and he held Mum's hand as she showed him round the house, smiling up at her sweetly. Twitchy, the traitor, purred herself round his feet and blinked kisses up at him.

She let him carry her round as if she was a soft toy, abandoning all her dignity.

When he'd gone, Molly asked us what we thought of him.

'Yes,' said Mum. 'He's gorgeous.'

'What do you think, Rosa?'

'Yes,' I said. 'He is.' But my heart was full and heavy with storm clouds, with deep down bottle green disappointment.

After six weeks of occasional visits and two sleepover weekends, Anthony moved in with his little brown suitcase, patchworked with stickers of teddy bears and dogs. For the time being he had the spare bed in my room, the one we'd bought for my new sister. Mum read him stories at night, and he sat with his thumb in his mouth and his eyes going glazy till he dropped off to sleep in her lap. She took two months' adoption leave off work and spent the time clearing out the spidery little spare bedroom, getting rid of her life's collection of books, clothes, the sewing machine that didn't work, the old computer, my broken dolls' house, paintings, all the stuff that might come in useful and which was now labelled 'junk'.

'Not the shoes,' I insisted.

'All right,' she said. 'We'll keep the shoes.'

The bag of shoes went back as far as Great-Grandma, who died when I was six. Lace-ups, heeled shoes, flat shoes, boots, zip boots, lace-boots, Velcro fastenings, little button fastenings, and every colour you could think of. Grandpa's slippers, with a hole under the right toe where he kept pressing the sustain pedal on the piano. Nana's little dancing pumps, soles worn threadbare from dancing at ceilidhs. When I looked at them I could imagine her, light-footed and laughing, dos-à-dos-ing and honouring her partner.

'They're a bit smelly,' Mum said, edging them towards the wastepaper basket.

'Don't you dare,' I said.

We found a box for them and stored them under my bed. Then she steamed off the wallpaper in the spare bedroom, singing every minute of the way, and took Anthony on a special trip to town and let him choose his own wallpaper. He chose Wallace and Gromit.

Grandpa adored him. He decided to come to the ice rink with Mum and me on Saturdays just so he and Anthony could learn to skate together. Anthony had no fear; within minutes he was out in the centre of the rink, tripping over his own skates, his legs scissoring and splaying, and he didn't care. By the end of the first session he was skating, really skating, a little brown blob with flashing feet, while Grandpa groped his way round the rink bar, clinging on for dear life. The new word for him is *stoical*.

It has to be said that everybody loved Anthony. The postwoman, the window cleaner, the woman next door, Sophie Baxter's mum, everyone. And if everyone loved him, what was wrong with me? I tried to make him cry, and it didn't work. I nipped him, and he pretended not to notice. I tipped his food away in the kitchen bin and he didn't care. It got worse. My one aim in life was to make Anthony cry.

Molly asked me if I was happy and I said yes. She looked at me for ages while I looked at her shoes, which were the square-toed sort that I don't like much, and she said, 'Are you still writing your diary, Rosa?'

'Sometimes,' I said, but it wasn't true. Somehow I'd lost heart when I knew I wasn't going to have a new sister.

'Good,' she said. 'It's important.'

As soon as she had gone I rummaged in my sock drawer and found the diary. I turned it upside down and opened it at the back page.

OK, Anthony, I wrote. I hate your grinning sweety-pie googie-eyed guts.

15
ABELA

Next day, Abela's breakfast remained untouched, but in the morning scramble nobody seemed to notice or to care. Mrs Sanderson arrived when the older children had already tumbled out of the house for their school bus or for work. She brought with her a warm jumper in the same cherry red that the other children in Abela's new school wore, and a grey pleated skirt, black woollen tights and lace-up shoes.

'You're a lucky girl,' she told Abela. 'Mrs Mount's little girl has just grown out of these, and she says you can have them. I'll take you to school this morning, and Carmel will fetch you home.'

Home! Abela's heart lurched at the word, but she looked gravely at Mrs Sanderson. She had come to expect disappointments. She already knew that home was a treacherous word; it meant many things. It was a word that kept slipping away and meaning something else. She dressed silently in her new clothes, hid her car and book under her pillow, and left the house with Mrs Sanderson, clopping along the pavement next to her in the stiff lace-up shoes that were heavier than her feet. *As long as I can still go to school,* she thought, *it will be all right.* She clenched her fists anxiously in the pockets of her new skirt, and only relaxed them when they turned a corner and at last she could hear the trilling sound of children's voices in the schoolyard.

'Off you go,' Mrs Sanderson said.

Jasmine skipped over to Abela as soon as she came through the gate, and they went into assembly together holding hands. *Today I am one of these children*, Abela thought, looking down proudly at her red and grey uniform. *Now I belong*. Nobody stared at her, nobody giggled. In class, Mister Hardy crouched by her table and asked her to read to him from a book with many words, which she did, slowly and bravely.

'That's very good,' he told her. 'You've been taught very well, Abela.'

'Soon I be doctor,' she told him. 'Go home, make people better.'

'I'm sure you will.' He stood up, giving a little grunt as his knees creaked. 'But you'll have to wait, oh, about twenty years before you're qualified. You'll have to work very, very hard.'

'I will work very, very hard,' she repeated the words joyfully. 'Then I go home.'

'Home to Tanzania. I've never been to your country,' he told her. 'Draw me a picture to show me what it's like.'

Abela thought for a long time before she took up any of the coloured pencils. She thought about her village, about the dusty red earth where children played and hens scratched, the sun striping through the trees where monkeys screamed and gibbered, the little vegetable plots and paddocks where skinny humpbacked cows lowed moodily to be milked. In the classroom around her, the other children worked at their various tasks, some of them whispering and giggling. She had forgotten about them, or where she was. She was so absorbed in her drawing that Jasmine had to shake her shoulder and take the coloured pencils away from her hand at the end of the afternoon.

'That's a funny house,' she said. 'It's good though.'

When the other children had run out to meet their parents, Abela still sat at her table, not knowing what to do or where to go. Mister Hardy came across and peered over her shoulder at the picture. It showed a round, thatched mud-red hut next to a tree that flamed with crimson flowers. Red and yellow swirls streaked the earth, and the sky was twisting with blue. A huge, yellow sun peered over a pointed mountain, vibrating with light and colour and life.

'This is Bibi's house,' she said.

'It's beautiful, Abela.' He held the picture up. 'Do you know, I can feel the heat throbbing up from the ground! Or is it the sand in the wind? There's so much movement!'

Abela only bobbed her head and laughed. She was so pleased with her picture that she wanted to stroke it.

'And who is Bibi?'

'My grandmother, Teacha,' she said softly.

Bibi, oh, Bibi. What are you doing now without me? Do you think about me?

Mister Hardy tiptoed quietly round her, clearing away his papers, tidying the classroom, just watching her without saying anything. All the other children had left by the time Carmel arrived.

'I'm always in a rush!' she laughed, her breath wheezing in tight little squeaks. 'How's she been? Not crying for her Carmel, I suppose?'

'She's been fine. She's been very busy,' Mister Hardy said. 'She's just finished a lovely picture.'

'Very nice,' she said. 'Is this for me?'

Abela looked anxiously at Mister Hardy, saying *no* with her eyes. *Please, no!*

'Hmm,' he said. 'It would be nice for the other children in the class to see where Abela lived. Perhaps we could put it up in the classroom here?'

He stuck it on the wall with Blu-Tack, and Abela looked at it, and then at him, her eyes wide and shining with pride. Mister Hardy was right. You could feel the dense, sticky blanket heat of home; you could feel the throbbing sun and the dusty swirl of sand. It was exactly right.

When they arrived back at the foster home, Carmel told Abela to run upstairs and change out of her school uniform before tea. In the girls' room she found some different clothes laid out for her on the bed; green trousers and a yellow sweatshirt. Lola and Cathy were in the room changing.

'Take your school clothes off,' Cathy said to her. 'You won't half be in trouble with old Ma Carmel if you don't.'

Abela ignored the new clothes, which she disliked, and put on her kanga, Mrs Long's cardigan, and Bibi's friend's sandals. Then she climbed onto her bed to look for her animal book. She wanted to carry on colouring now. Maybe Carmel had some coloured pencils that she could borrow. She could imagine the lion with flashes of black in his golden mane, as if it was lifting as he moved; swirls of air and sand around him. She opened the first page, the Simba page, and caught her breath in disbelief. She flicked over page after page. Every one had been scribbled on. The two girls watched her, raising their eyebrows at each other, pressing their hands against their mouths, shoulders shaking with suppressed laughter.

'My book!' Abela gasped, hugging it to her. 'My Susie book.'

'Her Susie book!' Lola snorted. 'Ah! Look, it's all spoiled. What a shame. Who'd have done that?'

Abela dived under her pillow for her car. It was missing. She slid off the bed, losing her balance in her panic, knocking her head on the ladder. The girls smirked at each other as she rummaged under all the beds, searching for the car.

'Where is my car!' she demanded.

'I don't know anything about a car,' Lola said. She was twisting Abela's beaded key-ring round and round in her fingers, looking at herself in the tiny mirror. 'Do you, Cathy?'

'No,' grinned Cathy. 'Haven't seen anything except that old tin can that fell out of the window.'

'Window,' repeated Abela. She ran to the window and looked out, and there it was, lying on the pavement below. 'My car!' she shouted.

One of Carmel's sons was coming down the street. He looked up when he heard Abela's voice, saw the car she was pointing at, and kicked it idly. It clattered into the gutter.

'Oi!' Lola shouted down to him. 'Don't leave no litter, ugly chops!'

The boy picked it up and Abela ran downstairs, her loose sandals clapping on the steps, and snatched the car off the boy. She hugged it to herself and refused to part with it, even when Carmel demanded to see it so she could find out what all the fuss was about.

'For goodness' sake!' the foster mother shouted. 'A battered old pop can! Wants chucking in the bin, that does. Kids, kids, kids. Maybe I've taken on one too many this time!'

Her husband growled something incomprehensible, and helped her to serve dinner for seven in the steamy, cluttered kitchen. Again, Abela refused to eat. She sat with her head down, stroking the Coca-Cola car that had been the best in her village.

'Eat,' Carmel demanded.

Abela moved the food round her plate with the back of her fork, and ate nothing.

At the end of mealtime Carmel took her upstairs, lifted her onto her bed, and scolded her loud enough for the entire household to hear.

'In this house, you eat what I give you to eat, do you understand? You wear what I tell you to wear, and you do what I tell you to do. Then we'll all get along very well.'

She repeated it every mealtime, every morning, every afternoon, and the other children would chorus after her, 'And we'll all get along very well, very well.' Carmel would stand with her hands on her hips, her big breasts wobbling, and scold and laugh and wheeze till tears streamed down her cheeks.

Abela didn't see her social worker again until the end of the week. Carmel called her downstairs and said that there was someone to see her, and she ran down eagerly, smoothing her green trousers and yellow sweatshirt, sure that it must be Bibi at last, at last, come all the way from Africa to take her home again. She was bitterly disappointed. She sat bleakly on the settee, head down, saying nothing, while Mrs Sanderson looked through all her notes and drank sweet tea with Carmel.

'How's she been?' the social worker asked.

'Sulky,' Carmel replied. 'She won't eat her food. But she's quiet enough, not like my other monsters,' she laughed. 'Like a zoo it is in here these days.'

'Are you happy here, Abela?' Mrs Sanderson asked her, when Carmel had gone outside to fetch some washing in. Abela nodded. If she said no, she might be taken away from the school, and she loved every minute of that.

'Where is Susie?' she asked.

'Susie's been in prison,' Mrs Sanderson told her. 'She

might have to go back, but she's gone to live with her parents, a long way from here. All right? Understand?'

'I want to see her,' Abela said.

'No,' Mrs Sanderson said firmly. 'I'm sorry, Abela. It's not possible. Be a good girl here. I'm trying to sort things out for you. And I don't want to move you away from the school.'

As long as I can go to school, Abela thought, *I will be all right.*

When she dressed for school again the next morning, Lola and Cathy shrieked with laughter. They didn't even bother to get out of bed. Ignoring them, Abela went down to breakfast.

'Oh, look at this eager beaver,' Carmel said to her husband. 'Get those school clothes off at once, child. No school today, nor tomorrow neither. Don't know what a weekend is?'

Abela had no idea what to do with herself. Lola and Cathy were allowed to go into town on Saturdays. 'Out of my hair,' Carmel said, and they piled out of the house full of giggles and high spirits, reeking of cheap perfume and hair mousse.

'Ah, peace at last!' Carmel said. 'Who'd be a foster mother? Who'd be a mother at all, come to think of it? I must be mad! You can make yourself useful, Abela, if you please. Help me do the beds. And we might go to the shops later. But you can't go out on your own. You're too little. You've got to stay home.'

Home. It was true. This was home, this place with red

161

carpet on the floor and echoey bedrooms and giggling girls and loud-voiced boys. It seemed it would be home for ever. Abela sat in the kitchen and worked through the book that Mister Hardy had given her to read, framing each word out loud until she had made sense of it. The Dad clattered through the dishes at the sink, then sat opposite her at the table, reading a newspaper. 'What's this say?' he growled to her a few times, and guffawed at her attempts to read the football news.

Abela went up to the bedroom. The house was so quiet now Lola and Cathy were out. It had a waiting hiss on its breath. She helped Carmel to change the sheets and then she climbed up and lay on her bunk. She could see out of the window at the wet London sky, the shiny lines of roofs one after another after another. Must she stay here for ever? A plane cruised silently across the sky, trailing a white plume behind it. Maybe it has come from Africa. She turned over onto her stomach, burying her face in her pillow. Please, please, please don't let Uncle Thomas be on that plane.

Every day, every night, she fretted that Uncle Thomas would come and beat her for getting Susie into trouble with the police. Her dreams were so real that she woke up sobbing, and Lola would thump the mattress from the bunk underneath to tell her to shut up.

'Leave her alone,' Cathy would mumble sleepily. 'She's only a kid.'

'She's an annoying brat,' Lola said. 'She gets on my tits.'

The two girls would howl with laughter till Carmel yelled through the door at them to cut it out.

At last the interminable weekend stretched to Monday and Abela was back in school. She learnt a song called 'January, February, March and April', telling all the months of the year. She couldn't stop singing it in her head; round and round it went, month after month, in a chant of children's voices. But the days crawled and the nights crawled, especially the time she spent at Carmel's house. Thoughts of Uncle Thomas haunted her. The only thing she enjoyed was school, but Mister Hardy noticed that she was often jumpy and frightened, especially if he ever raised his voice in order to speak to the whole class. One day he said, without looking at Abela,

'Children, if you're worried about anything, you know what to do, don't you?'

'Tell the worry box!' the children chanted, hardly looking up from the work they were doing.

'That's right. Post a letter in the worry box, if there's anything at all on your mind.'

For days Abela thought about this worry box, but didn't do anything. Every night Uncle Thomas broke into her dreams, shouting and slapping her with his big, damp hands. One day at break time when nobody was looking, she took a piece of paper and a pencil with her to the toilet. She knelt on the cold tiled floor in the cubicle and wrote, '*I am frade of Uncle Thomas. He beat me if you send me home. He want to sell me to rich fambly. I go to hell.*' She folded up the letter and walked,

163

trembling, to the worry box. No one was watching. She stood poised with the letter half in and half out of the slot. A door opened and Mister Helliwell came into the hall. She let go of the letter and ran out into the yard, and Jasmine came yelling up to her and grabbed her hands.

That afternoon Mister Hardy whispered to her that she need never worry about Uncle Thomas again. Her social worker came to see her after school and told her that she was very, very pleased that Abela had been able to write the letter to the worry box. Abela felt as if a cool hand was smoothing away the frown between her eyes.

'Would you like to tell me any more about your uncle?' Mrs Sanderson asked. 'You don't have to, if you don't want to.'

But Abela did want to. She told her about Uncle Thomas's wedding to Susie, and how quiet and strange and different it had been from any of the other village weddings she had seen. She told her about the airport, and how Uncle Thomas had made her wear a scarf to hide her face, and to walk with the Muslim women through the barrier. And she repeated what Susie had told her, that he was planning to sell her to a rich family, and it would be like going to Hell.

'I not bad girl, am I?' she finished. 'Bad girls go to Hell.'

Mrs Sanderson smiled and told her, no, she wouldn't go to Hell, and that she had been very brave to tell her all this. And from then, Abela began to relax, and stopped darting glances at the door or the window every now and again in case Uncle Thomas was there, waiting to punish her. Soon, instead, she replaced the bad dreams at night with good dreams, where Bibi came to see her. In her dreams, Bibi, not Uncle Thomas, was on the plane that rode through the sky. Bibi would find her way to Carmel's house. *Hodi, hodi,* she would call at the door, and Carmel would let her in and say nothing because she had never seen anyone so beautiful and smiling and confident before. Bibi would come into the bedroom and all the taunting and sniggering would stop because she had brought the scents of Africa with her. She would fold Abela in her arms. 'Come back with me now,' she'd say. 'It's time to go home.' Bibi would come.

'You know lots of English words now, Abela,' Mister Hardy told her. 'Nearly as many as English children of your age.'

'Are there many more words to learn?' she asked anxiously.

'Hundreds and hundreds,' he laughed. 'Hundreds of words that even I don't know.'

The thought of this mystified her. What kind of words could they be that even Mister Hardy didn't know? Where had they come from, and where would she find them? If she knew the names of everything in the world, would that use all the words up? And when all the words were used up, did someone make up more? She fell asleep at night trying to count the number of words she knew.

But too soon, it seemed, she was told that school was to be closed for the Easter holidays.

'Aren't you lucky?' Carmel said to her, spraying her as she laughed. 'You've only just got started, and it's the holidays already. Just don't get under my feet, any of you. Thank the Lord one of you at least is going away for Easter.'

'To Susie?' Abela asked.

'Not you. You can forget about Susie. But no school, Abela, for two whole weeks! Think of that!'

She couldn't bear to think of it. Two weeks without Mister Hardy or Jasmine. Two weeks of shouting Carmel and growling The Dad, of giggling, teasing nights, of listening to Cathy and Lola fighting and crying. Two weeks, she knew, were more than she could bear. She lay in bed watching the moonlight sliding over the rooftops like water, drowning the dark houses with silver light, and she knew what she wanted to do. She was frightened at the thought, but she knew she must do it. *Be strong, my kuku, be strong, be strong*.

She would go home to Bibi.

16
ROSA

It was the day of my level nine when everything went wrong. All night I dreamt about skating; in my dream I was as free and graceful as a swan, and at the end of the session the coach said I was so good that they were going to get me an audition for the big ice-dance show next month. It was going to be televised, and I would be the child star in it. I swooped gracefully round the rink, glittering with sequins, and all the people cheered.

Nothing like that happened.

I did not want Anthony to come skating with us that day. I asked Mum if he could stay with Nana, just this once. But Mum said that Grandpa wanted to give skating one last chance, so he and Anthony would definitely be coming too.

'What's wrong? Not nervous, are you?' she asked.

'A bit,' I said.

'Oh, Rosa, there's no need to be scared. It'll just be like an ordinary lesson. You'll sail through it. I'm the one who'll probably flop.'

She didn't understand. I wanted her to say, 'All right. Just me and you today, like old times.' But she didn't. Those old times had gone for ever.

So, I did something stupid. It was like the episode with Molly's boots. Once I get a silly idea in my head, I just go and do it. Act first and think later, that's Rosa, Nana says. This is what I did. While Mum was in the bathroom putting in her fiddly contact lenses, I got the kitchen scissors and snipped through one of the laces of my skating boots, nipped upstairs with it, and was standing outside the bathroom door wearing a look of total desolation when she came out.

'Look what he's done now!' I wailed, dangling the pink snipped-off lace like a dead worm between my finger and thumb. Anthony came out of his Wallace and Gromit room and stood next to me, gazing up at me, saying nothing at all.

And neither did Mum say anything at all. She simply went into her room and came back with her rusty Ebay skates, unlaced one of them, and handed the lace to me.

'Use that,' she said.

'But it's *black*!' I wailed. I could hear myself, I can hear it now, a silly little-spoilt-brat waily voice, and I couldn't do anything about it. 'It'll look awful on my pink boot.'

'She could have two black laces,' Anthony said helpfully. 'That would look better.'

'She can have one,' said Mum. 'And like it.'

Silently I collected my boots and skating skirt and followed Mum and Anthony down to the tram stop. Anthony was holding Mum's hand. He tried to hold mine, too, but I wasn't having any of that. No swinging

168

him between us like a shopping bag. I was still moaning inside myself.

When we arrived at the rink, Grandpa was waiting for us, full of grim determination. Anthony ran to him and flung his arms round Grandpa's legs, nearly toppling him over. Mum said she was going shopping, as she couldn't skate with only one boot.

'I'm sorry, Mum,' I said, and she gave me a quick hug.

'Good luck,' she said. 'You'll be fine.'

I watched her go, and my despair trudged after her like a shadow. I needed her with me that day.

And I didn't feel fine. I felt like a freak, with my pink skirt and pink headband and red-heeled boots and one black lace. And it was all my own stupid bratty fault. I didn't want to skate after all; I just wanted to run after Mum and tell her the truth about the lace. I wanted her to shout at me enough to make me cry, and then to forgive, to put her arms round me and hug me again, really tightly. But the time for that had passed.

'Ready?' Grandpa grinned at me. He wasn't feeling as brave as he looked, I could tell that, and that gave me a bit of courage. We all stepped onto the ice together, stoical Grandpa shook hands with us both ceremoniously as if he never expected to see us again, then I went off to my level nine class, Anthony whisked himself over to level two, and Grandpa shuffled and wobbled to the beginners.

I took a deep breath. *Rise above it*, I told myself. *Put it all behind you*. Nana talk, that. I could just hear her.

Think about now, go for the *now moment*. That's the sort of thing she says. *Now* is the time that matters. OK, Nana. And somehow, it worked. I did everything right. I was a swan. But Mum wasn't there, and I didn't feel any kind of elation. Someone had stolen it away from me.

It was when we were doing the free skating as the public was coming in that the worst thing and the best thing happened. I noticed that Mum had come in. She was sitting near the café with her flask on the table and, I was sure, our muesli bars. I waved to her and began to float, languidly, effortlessly, my very best skating. She would know I had passed, and this was for her, just for her. Then I heard Anthony shouting my name. He was skating towards me, in that knees-out, elbow-waving, froggy way of his, shouting over the canned music and pointing at my boots. I was furious. He was spoiling my moment for Mum. Did he want everyone to notice my one black lace? Did he want to ruin it all for me, making everyone laugh at me? I turned my back on him.

'Rosa, look at your boots! Look at your lace!'

I ignored him. I stretched one leg behind me and did a slow spin round, just for Mum, building it up, building it up, faster, faster.

'Rosa!' Anthony shouted at the top of his voice. 'Look!'

And I did look, and I was too late.

One of my laces, the black traitor lace, had come unfastened and had coiled itself round my blade. As I spun, it locked. I lost my balance, crashed over, and a pain like broken glass sliced through my ankle.

People came rushing to lift me up, but Anthony was there first. He was crying. For the first time since I had met him, he was crying. He knelt on the ice, holding my hand in both of his, and the tears were streaming down his cheeks. Two men skated over to me and carried me off the ice, and Mum came running from the café area, white and anxious, and people clustered round, but in all that time Anthony never let go of my hand, never stopped crying. Somebody brought a car to the emergency exit to take me to the accident unit at the Hallamshire hospital, and he ran along beside me as they were carrying me out. I leaned over and hugged him.

'Don't worry, Anthony,' I said, smoothing his face, wiping his tears away. 'I'll be fine.'

Anthony and I had a lot of fun together while my ankle was getting better. We did the *Lord of the Rings* jigsaw that Nana bought for me, and played some crazy computer games. We watched some totally surreal Japanese animations on DVD. I read stories to him, and he and I enjoyed it so much, that closeness, that wonder of story, that I decided to teach him to read. It was the best thing I have ever done, hearing him saying the letters as I pointed them out to him, watching him frown as he tried to make sense of whole words, seeing his face light up as he came to the end of a little sentence and understood it all. Soon he was reading to me, faltering and glancing up at me every now and then to make sure he was getting it right, simple words, but he was getting there, and then I would take over and read him some of the wonderful stories that Mum used to read to me.

I love reading, I love words, I hoard them and gloat over them the way I gloat over shoes. I love books. And now I've passed on that love to someone else. Now I know how Grandpa feels when we're playing the piano together, and we make music out of what just looks like a dance of dots and tadpoles on a page. *Richer*, that's how I feel.

Anthony's social worker and Molly came round quite a few times, and it was obvious that they were both really pleased with the way things were going. Then came the big day, nearly three months after Anthony started to live with us; the apricot slices and red shiny shoes day, when they both came together. Of course, Molly had talked to Mum and me about this already, and Anthony's social worker had already talked to him. We knew what question was going to be asked, and they knew what answer was going to be given. But it was still achingly nerve-wracking, for all of us. I was a bag of jitters. We tidied the room as if we were expecting Prince Harry to pop in. Anthony helped to set the tray for tea. We lit the fire. Mum had filled the room with daffodils. It was a few days before Easter, and the sun was full of hail and the rain was full of blue skies, that sort of day. And Molly said,

'Well, Jen and Rosa. You've been having a lovely time with Anthony. Would you like to tell him what you told me earlier? Would you like him to be a member of your family?'

Mum and I dared to look at each other. Her eyes were sparkly, and I should think mine were too. My throat felt as if an apple was stuck in it.

'Yes, please,' I said.

'Yes,' said Mum. 'We would, wouldn't we, Rosa?'

Anthony's social worker said to him, 'And how about you, Anthony? Can you remember what you said to me this morning? Would you like Jen to be your new mummy, and Rosa to be your new sister? Would you like to grow up in this family?'

Anthony's eyes were as round as plates. He looked solemnly from one to the other of us, as if he was reaching deep down inside his thoughts to a place where none of us had ever been. I was begging him inside my head, 'Say yes, say yes, Anthony.' My fists were clenched tight round my knees.

'Yes,' he said.

17
ABELA

I ran away on Easter Sunday. We had painted eggs for breakfast. Lola had gone to spend the weekend at her cousin's hotel, and Cathy was very upset about this. She sat at the table sniffing noisily, bashing her boiled egg with a spoon until Carmel took it away from her and threatened to send her to bed like a naughty little girl. The younger of the Oladipo boys had been given a chocolate egg by the man at the paper shop where he worked on a Saturday, and Carmel told him he must share it with us. He sulkily broke one of the halves into little pieces and passed them round. I watched him out of the corner of my eye, but he didn't give any to me. I didn't care. He was the one who had kicked my car into the gutter.

Carmel went to church, and took her sons and Cathy with her. I would love to go, I would love to sing with all the people like we used to do at home, to listen to the rainbow of sound and slide my own voice into it, my yellow voice. I had not heard my voice singing out loud for months and months. But I knew that this was my chance and I said no, so she shook her head at me and told me to stay in my room and say my prayers instead. The Dad growled at me to say them quietly because he was listening to a cricket match on the radio.

I went upstairs and put my blue kanga on, then wrapped up my poor scribbled-in book and my battered car in my spare one. I left my school uniform and the tights and shoes neatly on my bunk, and I wrote a little note for the secretary. '*Dere Mis Mownt. Thank for the very nice clothe. I hope a notha girl like them too.*'

Then I went. The Dad had fallen asleep over his cricket match; his snores rumbled like thunder.

I walked out of the house and closed the door softly, so softly, behind me. I was going to Bibi.

18
ROSA

Then things went wrong. Maybe it was Molly's fault, who knows, but it was a terrible, terrible sad thing. What Molly had told us was that Anthony's actual adoption day in County Court would be a mere formality, a signing of papers. Nothing could go wrong now, she promised us. So when her car drew up outside the house one Saturday morning we thought nothing of it. Grandpa was with us, collecting Anthony for his first fishing trip. My ankle was much better but it still wasn't strong enough for me to go skating, the physio had said. *Fizzio*, Mum and I call him, so we think of him as being someone light and frothy to make me giggle instead of making me wince with pain with all the exercises he gives me to do. Anyway, instead of going skating on her own, Mum decided that she and I could assemble the Ikea cupboard she had bought to put in Anthony's bedroom. I could do with a new cupboard too, but I didn't say anything.

Molly came to the door as Anthony and Grandpa were standing there, and her face was full of woe. It told us everything, though she waited till the fishing party had left before she said anything.

'I'm afraid I've got some bad news for you,' she said.

'The worst case scenario,' Mum said bleakly. I had no idea what she meant by that.

'Anthony's father has been in touch with us. I'm afraid, I'm so very, very sorry ...'

'He wants him back.' Mum's voice was so flat, so empty of colour and shape, that it was like a ghost voice. I could hardly hear her.

Molly nodded. I thought she was going to cry. I'm sure she felt like it. 'Anthony's social worker rang me last night. I've been with him to see the father this morning. He's come back to live in Sheffield, because he can't bear to be without Anthony any longer. His marriage is over. I'm afraid you're right. He realises he's made a terrible mistake. He wants his little boy back.'

'But he can't have him back,' I shouted, full of outrage, full of passionate, hopeless, helpless anger. 'He's no right to have him back! Not now.'

'He has every right,' Molly said sadly. 'He's Anthony's father. We could try to fight it, but I'm afraid we wouldn't win. By law, he has every right.'

I will never forget that day. I will never forget the day Anthony stood silently by the front door with his little brown suitcase and his fishing rod from Grandpa in his hand. I will never forget the knock that told us that his social worker had come for him. But when Mum opened the door, the social worker was sitting in his car and a strange man was standing on the doorstep; Anthony dropped the rod and ran to him and the man bent down and swung him up and they hugged each other as if they would never, ever let each other go.

'Daddy, Daddy,' Anthony kept saying. 'Daddy, my daddy.'

The man's eyes were closed. His face was wet.

19
ABELA

Just after I left Carmel's house, I saw something wonderful. It was a strange animal, red with a bushy tail. I don't think anyone else saw him as he sniffed and dipped along the street. He was like a dog, but not a dog. He was like the *jackal-bweha* that howls around the desert places of home, but not a *jackal-bweha*. And when he paused and looked at me with one foot lifted, ready for flight, I went cold and wondering with the thrill of seeing him, and I remembered the lions flickering past me in the night forest. I felt my mother and father standing behind me with their hands on my shoulders, and I felt calm again. Be brave, be brave, their whispers told me, and the red fox slipped away.

I took deep, slow breaths, as if the air was liquid and I was drinking it down to fill up my lungs. It was the first time I had been on my own since the day I left Susie's flat and ran to the school, following the dream trail of children's voices. Today there was no trail. I had no idea where to go. I looked up at the sky, squinting at the sharp light of the sun. I could hear the sound of a plane up there, the big silver bird that flew free. Maybe Bibi was on that plane, looking down, full of wonder because now she knew how big the world was. Maybe I

179

should go back to the house and wait for Bibi. *But I have waited for Bibi for weeks and months. It is time for me to go to her.*

So I started to run, glancing up every now and again to keep the plane in sight so I would know which way to go, but I had not gone very far when a strange man stopped me. He just stepped out in front of me, blocking my way. He had red hair, like the fox, and his face was sharp and thin as if the wind had carved it. He put out his hand to stop me and gripped my shoulder. Then he lifted up my chin and smiled down at me.

'What a pretty girl!' he said.

I squirmed away. I did not know what to say to him. I was losing my plane; it dipped from sight behind his head. I tried to squirm away but his grip on my shoulder tightened. I wanted to run past him, but I was afraid that if I did, he would follow and hound me back to Carmel's house.

'Where are you going to, my pretty maid?' he asked, in a strange, lilting voice like a child singing a song.

But I was ready for that question. I had the answer all ready in my head, the words laid out like a string of bright beads. I had been saying them to myself for many days now. 'London, Heathrow Airport, Africa, Tanzania,' I chanted. And in my head I added, 'Bibi's house,' but that was too magic to say aloud. That would be like breaking a spell.

'All that way!' he laughed, cocking his head from side to side. 'I hope you've got your passport.'

My passport! I had forgotten all about that little book with my shy photograph inside it. It must still be in Susie's flat, in that cupboard underneath the television set where she kept her clutter of things. I broke away from the man and started to run – now at least I knew where I was going, because I had seen Susie's flat many times on my way to the shops with Carmel. Sometimes I would stop and look at it longingly, wondering if Susie was still there. Susie was my only link with home; she knew Bibi's house, she could take me there if she wanted to. Maybe the social worker with hair like feathers was wrong, maybe Susie was still there, waiting to take me home.

I could hear the man following me as I ran, calling me to wait because he knew how to help me, and I dodged across the road so a big red bus blundered between me and him, and then I darted up a side street towards the flats. I banged on the door, and when nobody answered I kicked it till my feet hurt, and at last the woman from the downstairs flat opened it up. Her big belly had gone, and she was holding a baby in one arm. She glared down at me.

'You again! What're you after?'

'Please, Teacha, I want Susie,' I said. The baby clenched and unclenched his fist, wrapping his fingers round with the woman's hair.

'No Susie here,' the woman said, uncoiling the baby's fingers. 'Gone. Couple of months ago. Didn't you know?'

So it was true. She started to close the door, and I

tried to edge inside, to slide like a cat through the gap that she had left.

'No, you don't,' she said.

'Please, I go to her flat,' I pleaded.

'No way,' she shouted, and the baby started scream-ing. 'Look what you done now. Clear off. Can't have you wandering all over the place. There's new people up there now. Nice people.'

'Please, I want my passport.' I could hardly make myself heard over the screaming of the baby; its voice spiralled like knives round the concrete hall and stairs.

'There's nothing of yours there, I tell you. Oh, hang on—' She stepped back and picked an envelope off a pile of letters by the stair. 'Is this you – Abela Mbisi?'

She said it wrong, but I knew my name. I reached out and grabbed the blue envelope from her and hugged it to my chest in case she tried to take it back again.

'It come through the post weeks ago. Well, I didn't know where to send it, did I? People come and go, I can't keep track of them. Now clear off.' She hitched the baby onto her shoulder and gave me a shove with her free arm. 'You don't belong here no more.'

She shut the door on me. The screams of the baby still jangled in my ears as I turned away, desolate now, and slumped down onto the step. I put my bundle down and tore open the letter. There was no passport there, just a sheet of blue paper with some scrawled writing on it that I couldn't read. A hand reached out to touch my cheek and I jumped up. It was the man who had followed me before.

'Oh dear, she wasn't very nice, was she?' he said, his voice so drooling with kindness that it made me want to cry.

'I want my passport,' I sniffed, trembling to hold back the sobs that were welling up inside me. *Be strong, be strong, Abela.* Don't cry in front of strangers. I picked up my things and shoved the letter into the middle of the bundle, where it would be safe for me to try to decipher later. I turned away from the man and started to walk down the road. Maybe if I got to Heathrow Airport everything would be all right. I could tell the people there that Susie had my passport, and maybe they would let me get on the plane anyway. I could tell them my uncle in Africa would pay for my ticket. They would let me go home, surely they would let me go home to Bibi.

I had only gone a few steps when the man caught up with me. 'London, Heathrow Airport, Africa, Tanzania,' he was singing, 'Hey ho, a long way to go! Want me to help you?'

I stopped, clutching my bundle tightly, both arms wrapped round it. 'Can you?' I asked. There was hope in his words, a bright bird of hope fluttering its wings at me. He swung himself in front of me and then he looked down, smiling, cocking his head to one side like a wise bird.

'Of course I can help you. Come with me. I can take you to Heathrow Airport. I can help you to get that magic thing, you know, that passport? Can't go without that, but I can help you.' He held out his hand. His voice was so kind. His mouth was so smiley.

But I looked up into his eyes and saw that he was not smiling inside. How could this be? I did not understand this man, and I did not understand why I was afraid of him. He was giving me hope; my palm trees and my green monkeys, my dusty red earth, my Bibi. If I took his hand, all these things would be mine. But when I looked into his eyes I was more frightened of him than I ever was of the mad mzee swinging her panga to chop off my head in the market place. I was more frightened of him than of the lions who walked by me in the jungle. I backed away from him and turned; I started running, faster, faster than I have ever run in my life. I could hear his feet drumming behind me, his long legs stretched, his long arm reaching out to haul me back. I could hear his voice calling, 'Come back, child, come back. I'm not a bad man. I want to help you. I want to help you.'

I am good at running. I can run fast. I can run for miles and miles and never get tired. I can run in the sweltering heat of Africa. My feet belong to the earth; they are part of it. Long after I heard the man's feet slowing down, long after I heard his voice growing fainter and his breath heaving, long after I couldn't hear him at all, I kept on running. That running was like being free, like turning into a bird, it was like flying. I left everything behind. I left the man with the cruel eyes and the smiling face, I left him so far behind that I did not know whether he had really been there at all, or whether he was a bad magic dream. I left my happy school and my best friend Jasmine and my special

184

teacher; I left scolding Carmel and The Dad who growled in his belly, and the big girls who hated me. I left it all behind, fear and hope together; I ran and ran until there was nothing left to run away from. When I stopped, I was weak with hunger and tiredness. I had no idea where I was. I saw a garden with a shed in it, the door swinging open, and I crept inside. I dropped onto my hands and knees, and then I sank onto the wooden floor. I folded up my bundle to make a pillow, and saw again the blue letter with my name written on the envelope. I have never had a letter before. Still lying there, I opened the letter and little by little, I began to untie the tangled sprawl of words.

It wasn't until the next afternoon that Abela was found, when the son of the owner of the house came to the shed to fetch his bicycle. He backed out again and ran into the house, where his mother was smearing white paint over the green wall of her bedroom, humming along to a pop song on the radio.

'Mum!' he shouted. 'Mum! MUM!' She turned and looked at him in astonishment as he ran into the bedroom and switched off the radio so she would hear him. 'There's a dead girl in the shed.'

His mother dropped the brush so paint smeared the floorboards like a white exclamation mark of horror. She ran down the stairs after her son. Together they paused, and together they stepped into the shed, where the little crumpled bundle of a child lay.

'Get the police!' the mother said hoarsely. She knelt down, her heart fluttering with fright, and touched the child's cheek. It was warm. She was alive. With a sob of relief the woman lifted Abela up and carried her into the house.

'I think she's unconscious,' she told her son. 'We need a doctor. Or an ambulance. Or maybe' – she watched as Abela's hands tightened round the blue envelope – 'maybe she's just in a deep, deep sleep.'

The police and the ambulance arrived at the same time. There was a major search on for a child who had been reported missing by her foster parents, so the policewoman phoned the social services immediately to tell them that a child answering Abela's description had been found in a shed, several miles from home, and that she appeared to be unharmed but in a state of exhaustion. They decided to send Abela to hospital for observation and there she stayed, deeply asleep between the stiff white sheets of the hospital bed, like the sleeping beauty in the forest. In the locker next to the bed were her clothes, a battered car made out of a Coca-Cola tin, a dog-eared exercise book, and a crumpled blue letter.

When she eventually woke up she found two women sitting on either side of the bed, watching her intently. One was the woman with hair like white feathers. The other was a stranger but not a stranger; a woman out of her dreams with loose hair the colour of lions. I know you, Abela wanted to say, but she was too tired to speak. This woman leaned forward and stroked Abela's hand and spoke to her softly in her own language, the language of hot sun and dry winds, the language of home. Abela opened her eyes again and listened, saying nothing, and it was as if she was listening to a song. Then she drifted back into a calm sleep.

When she woke up again it was a different time of day, maybe a different day. She could hear rain like tiny drumbeats against the window. She closed her eyes again and lay listening to it. It was a sweet sound. Then she focused in on two voices. Some of the words were familiar. Some of them meant nothing at all. She didn't try to understand, just listened to the words.

'I don't know why she would run away from the Oladipos,' one voice, the familiar feather voice said. 'They're one of our best foster parents.'

'I agree. They're brilliant with difficult teenagers. But this child isn't a difficult teenager. She's a child lost in the wrong country. She needs a lot of gentle care.'

'Maybe we should move her to a different home?'

'I don't think so, not yet. It's not the right time to make changes. And now there's the letter.'

Abela opened her eyes at once. She looked wildly around her.

'What is it, Abela?' the woman with lion hair asked her in Swahili.

'My letter.'

'Don't worry. I have the letter. Soon, we'll read it together. When you're better.'

Abela stared up at her. She was sure now that she had

187

seen her before. She recognised her smell now, and the way her hair fell softly around her face. She knew her, for sure. She struggled to bring the memory up. It was like a fish, looming slowly and surely out of the murky depths of a river to rise, at last, into light. She had it. 'You give me money,' she blurted out.

'Money!' Mrs Sanderson said. 'Why do you want Miss Carrington to give you money, Abela?'

Abela ignored her. 'Miss Carrington,' she murmured. It was a nice name.

'What is it?' Miss Carrington spoke to her in her own language.

'You came to my country. You gave me money to make my mother better. You were on the bus.'

'Good heavens!' Miss Carrington looked across at Mrs Sanderson. 'Would you believe it, Tessie, I know this child already! I met her right at the very beginning of my visit to Tanzania, months ago!' She turned back to Abela. 'What happened to your mother?'

'She died,' Abela whispered.

Miss Carrington closed her eyes and sighed. She remembered the day, of all the days she had spent in East Africa. She remembered the frightened child and her brave, dignified mother. She remembered her feeling of helplessness as she watched the two make their slow, difficult way from the bus to the hospital. Now she was back from her travels, her temporary replacement Tessie Sanderson was handing back her caseload. She had come to the hospital with her that day simply because Tessie

Sanderson had told her that Abela was Tanzanian, and it might help her to have someone to speak to her in her own language. She had worked in Arusha some years ago. She knew Swahili well.

Abela at last drifted off to sleep, and Judith Carrington and Tessa Sanderson left together.

'You're not leaving for another month, but I'll take this child on now,' Miss Carrington said. 'I think she needs some pretty intensive support, and I think it should start straight away. I'll take her back to Mrs Oladipo's tomorrow and try to make things easier for her there. And I'll talk to her about the letter.'

I do not want to go back to the Carmel-lady house, but Miss Carrington tells me she's a good kind lady and I'll be happy there now. I tell her I'm frightened of the big girls.

'They've not been very nice to you,' she frowned. 'But I'll talk to them, and Mrs Oladipo will talk to them. They're lonely, you see. They've lost their mums and dads too. They've had a bad time.'

I say nothing. I stare out of the window of her car and I watch the great buses and trucks. When we come to the house, Mrs Oladipo gives me a hug, warm and soft like pillows, and Mr Oladipo he growls in his belly and even his mouth turns up and his teeth show to make a smile.

'I've moved her things,' Carmel says to Miss Carrington. 'When Abela first came I thought it would be a good idea to put her in with Lola and Cathy, give her someone to talk to, but I can see now it didn't work. I'd no idea what was going on up there. So, you've got your own room now, Abela,' she says to me. 'My big lad's got himself a job in Gravesend, so you can have his room for a while. Come and have a look.'

I love my new room. It has yellow yellow sunshine walls, and lots of pictures, happy pictures, happy children.

'These are all my children,' Mrs Oladipo laughs. 'All the children who've stayed in the house with me and Tomi. Do you want your picture here, Abela?'

I keep my head down but I make it nod. My only picture is in the passport book that has disappeared somewhere.

'Well, we only have smiling children on the wall here, so when your lovely big smile comes back, we'll get the camera out. Now, are you hungry?'

I make my head nod again.

'Good girl. Just for tonight, you can have your tea early, before Lola and Cathy have theirs. They're talking to Miss Carrington first. They'll be good girls now, I tell you. But from tomorrow, we eat together, we're a family again.'

And she bends down and hugs me cuddly soft again, and I never had that hug since I said, 'Bye-bye, Bibi'. I don't hug back; I keep my arms stiff like trees.

Then she takes me down and I eat my tea and The Dad growls and chuckles and watches TV while I eat, and then he switches it off and goes out to mow the grass and the house is sweet with a green smell that comes through the windows. Miss Carrington comes back from upstairs where she's been talking to Lola and Cathy, and they follow her down and look at me like sheep through their floppy hair.

'Hi, Bella, how're yer doing?' Lola says, sloppy with chewing gum.

'Glad you're better, Bella,' Cathy says.

I say nothing. I don't look back at them. They go in the kitchen and eat their tea all on their own. Miss Carrington and Mrs Oladipo sit with me on the settee and Miss Carrington opens her bag and brings out my blue letter.

'Have you read this, Abela?' she asks me, and I make my head nod again, but I don't look at her or at anything. I am watching the window where the sound of mowing is coming from but I am not seeing anything.

'I'm going to read it out loud,' she says. 'I want Mrs Oladipo to hear it, and I want to make quite sure that you understand every word. When I've read it in English for you both, I will read it again in Kiswahili, and then we will talk about it. OK?'

I nod again. I bite my lip because I know it will shake. I close my hands tight like knots of rope round my knees. I do not want to hear the words again.

'It's from Susie,' Miss Carrington explains to Mrs Oladipo. 'She sent it to the flat for Abela. I suppose she thought it would eventually reach her through the social services.' She makes her throat do a tiny cough. '*Dear Bella, I hope someone sends this to you. I don't know where they've taken you. I have bad news for you. I'm*

191

sorry I haven't been a good person to you but I'm not your mother and I shouldn't have pretended I was your mother. I was wrong to do that. Your Uncle Thomas is not coming to England. He is not allowed to come. That is why I married him and why I pretended to be your mum, so he could come here. I think you should go back home now. But I have very bad news for you. Your Uncle Thomas has told me on the phone that your grandmother has died of malaria. I am very sorry. Love, Susie.

When Miss Carrington finishes reading the letter in English Mrs Oladipo says, 'Oh my God,' and holds my hand. Miss Carrington reads the letter in Swahili and I understand some bits better, but the bit at the end I know already, I have understood all those words. I have understood that I will never, never be happy again.

Judith Carrington had to wait until the next case conference was held before she could discuss Abela with her team leader, Denis, and the other members of his team. She told them how Abela had run away from her foster home to try to get back to Tanzania, and how she had been taken to hospital after being found in a traumatised state in a shed.

'Was she unhappy at this foster home?' the team leader asked, frowning.

'It wasn't ideal,' Judith admitted. 'She had to be taken to a place of safety when the woman she was living with was arrested, and the Oladipos had a spare place. I think also that my colleague chose to send Abela there in the first place because the Oladipos are black.'

'But aren't they Nigerian?'

'I believe so.'

Denis rubbed his hands across his hair, making it sit up in thoughtful spikes, then smoothed it down again. 'Sending a Tanzanian child to a Nigerian foster home because they're all black makes as much sense as sending a Russian child to a French home because they're white,' he murmured. 'Anyway, so you sent her back to them after she left hospital.'

'I did. At least it was familiar. I believed she would make progress with them.'

Denis glanced down at the notes, reminding himself of the facts. 'So she's an immigrant?'

'Possibly illegal, almost certainly an orphan,' Judith said.

'And *has* she made progress?'

Judith sighed. She had been a social worker for fifteen years, apart from the year off she had just given herself. In all that time she had seen many children in desperate situations. She never grew hardened to their plight, but she did learn to distance herself. But Abela had touched her in a way that no other child had. 'She's been through an awful time. She's had nightmares, cried a lot. I've been visiting her every week for six weeks and now I'm working with Mrs Oladipo to help her through her grief.'

'How is she coping with it?'

'She understands that she'll never see her family again. She's let go of that longing. But she needs to have something to put in its place. Hope.' She didn't need to utter the word, surely. She was with people who understood how important and how fragile hope was.

'No living relatives?'

'She has an uncle. She's very frightened of him. She put a letter in the school worry box to say that he wanted to sell her.' Judith riffled through some more papers and put them on Denis's desk. 'I think it's probably true. I've done some investigating...there's confirmation here that he was deported from England over a year ago and will never be allowed to return – he had no work permit and there is unconfirmed suspicion that he was involved in child trafficking.'

'So she can't go to him,' Denis agreed. 'What do you recommend, Judith?'

Judith leaned forward eagerly, glancing round at her colleagues. 'I recommend that Abela should be allowed to stay in England in the care of the social services. I think she should be placed for adoption as soon as possible.'

She sat back and closed her eyes, and she felt again the sweltering heat of the African sun, the chant of excited voices as boys ran to greet her bus with their trays of fruit and cakes, and the little girl holding a strip of material over her mother's head to give her some shade. She could hear her colleagues murmuring round her, discussing Abela's case. None of them knew Abela, yet her future was in their hands.

At last the committee came to a decision. They agreed that Abela should be placed for adoption, but not that she should be kept in England.

'It's not in her best interests,' Denis said, as Judith started to protest. 'She's only lived here for six months. I think we agree.' He glanced round at the others in the team. 'We should make arrangements for her to be repatriated so that the Tanzanian social services can place her for adoption in her own country.'

Judith Carrington could have cried with frustration.

20
ROSA

Cats *know* when their owners are unhappy. It's uncanny. Our Twitchy, totally independent, freeloading, who-do-you-humans-think-you-are, you're-just-here-to-feed-me attitude, just changed completely after Anthony went. She started to sit on Mum's knee without being invited, purr like a tractor, do cute dabby-paws things with passing spiders just to make us smile. She never behaves in such an undignified way usually. Then one day she disappeared for a week. When we found her again in the drawer of an old filing cabinet that was going rusty in the coal-hut, she had become the proud mother of four unbelievably tiny kittens. Pink-mouthed, wobbly-legged, stretchy, yawny, blinky and totally absorbing. I could watch them for hours, forget homework, no problem. We named them Little Chap, Wonky Tail, Belly-burster and Fancy Pants, and we were crazy about them all. We had a riotous time while they lived with us; they chased everything in sight, including their own tails; they rolled on top of each other and cuffed each other; they scrambled inside my school bag, curled up inside flowerpots; they had no idea how to be good, and they just played from sleep-time to sleep-time. When they were eight weeks old Mum said we had to find homes for them. She wouldn't listen to my pleadings – 'No, we can't have five cats, no, not four, not three, not even two. I mean it, Rosa.'

So I found homes for them, all with kids from school, which was quite neat because it meant that I would be able to visit them. Their new owners named them Freddy, Nutmeg, Beatrix and Sheba and lugged them away in cat boxes, taking all that fun and wonder away with them. So we were alone again, and the house felt empty, and that night Twitchy prowled round all the rooms howling deep in the back of her throat for the kittens she had lost.

During this time Molly visited us again. We never really expected to see her again, which was sad because I had come to really like her, with her faded, hippy clothes and her spectacular shoes. But after Anthony left, we put all thoughts of adoption behind us. We had tried and failed, Mum said. Never again.

'You mustn't say that,' Nana told her. 'Never say never again. Just think, Jen – twelve months before you were born, I had a miscarriage. It felt like the end of the world. I had grown to love that baby inside me so much. She died when I was six months pregnant. It was a terrible experience, wasn't it, Charles?'

Grandpa nodded and cleared his throat abruptly, as if he'd suddenly thought of a tune he wanted to hum. His fingers tapped on the tabletop.

Nana put her hands over his, stopping the silent arpeggio he was playing.

'That's it now, I thought,' she went on. 'I'm never going to try again. I can't put myself through all that grief again. But I did. We did.' She glanced at Grandpa, and they exchanged the slightest flicker of a smile. 'It took a lot of courage, but we tried again. And if we hadn't – just think! You would never have been born.'

But Mum could only look inside herself. She wouldn't go into Anthony's room with its Wallace and Gromit wallpaper. She had a photograph of him in there, but she wouldn't go in to look at it, not that I knew of, anyway.

So when Molly came round, Mum greeted her politely and asked her in, but she didn't offer her a cup of tea, and they didn't chat like old friends. I know she blamed Molly because the adoption had fallen through; I think she felt that if Molly had been more thorough, Anthony would never have been placed for adoption in the first place.

'I've just come to see if you'd like me to keep your name on the books,' Molly said.

I clenched and unclenched my fingers. And Mum said no. She didn't look at me, didn't look at Molly. Her face was white.

'That's it then,' said Molly, closing up her folder. 'Gosh, the end of the story. I'm so sorry, Jen. You have a lot to offer. Let me know if you ever change your mind.'

'I won't,' Mum said. 'That's it now.'

But life is full of little miracles, Nana says, and not long after all that, something totally unexpected happened, and it's changed our lives again.

It started with a phone call, one blissful Saturday when I was just setting off to skate. It was my first time since the accident; my broken ankle had taken ages to heal, and the doctor said I must be very careful or I'd do myself permanent damage. So I was nervous about going, even though I was dying to get back into skating again, but Mum and Grandpa said they'd go with me. The phone rang just as I was sorting out my things in my room. I had gone off the Barbie pink stuff, totally and utterly. Leave them to the five-year-olds. I just chose the black tracksuit trousers I use for games at school, and an olive-green sweatshirt that used to be Mum's. I didn't want to shine, not any more. I wanted to blend in with the crowd, not be noticed, not be seen.

'Oh, brilliant!' I heard Mum say as I ran downstairs. 'That'll be really wonderful. I'll look forward to it.'

She put the receiver down and swung round to me. Her eyes were shining, and her voice was happier than it had sounded for ages.

'Who was that?' I asked.

'Never you mind. A surprise. You'll find out. Quick now, we mustn't be late.' And that was all she'd say, though her face kept dimpling into smiles.

Grandpa was waiting for us outside Ice Sheffield as usual. She linked her arm in his and skipped him through the door, which is something I've never seen her do before. Grandpa raised his eyebrows at me and

I shrugged. Perhaps she's in love, I thought wildly. Perhaps she's got a boyfriend!

Well, then I forgot about Mum and her peculiar cheerfulness, because I was really nervous about going skating again and it was all I could do to get myself laced up and ready for action. Mum and Grandpa held my hands when we stepped onto the ice, then he let go and flapped to the side, saying he was bound to fall over and bring me tumbling down with him. He tottered round slowly, his arms windmilling out and round in his efforts to stay upright, whistling to himself to show how carefree he felt. I knew his heart was thumping as loudly as mine was.

Mum kept hold of my hand and we did a whole circuit together, slow and steady, and then she said, 'You'll be fine, off you go now.' She let go and I was free; I could do it, I was myself again. Paige twisted and shimmered in her new dove-lilac outfit, smiling graciously at me. I heard the screech of Jamie's ice hockey blades behind me, and then he streaked past, hands flapping hello. He yelled to me to race him. Toby tore after him, head down, grunting with the effort of keeping up, and I shrieked, 'Yeehah!' and pushed myself off after them both. It was a great feeling, skimming in and out between the other skaters; I felt completely confident again. I slowed down to get my breath back, and did a gentle spin, and that was when I saw the little boy in the middle of the rink, right in the glowing square of sunlight that came through the window. He had no style whatsoever. He was completely fearless. He was laughing across at me. I could hardly believe it; I daren't believe it.

I glanced over to where Mum was skating with her friend Pat. She saw me and waved, and I pointed. She saw him too, her face lit up, and we both skated towards him.

'Anthony!' I shouted.

He flung his arms wide, lunging towards me like a dog let off its leash, and I just caught him before he catapulted into me. I lifted him right up and hugged him, tight, tight. We were all laughing, Anthony, me and Mum, and then the man who I recognised as Anthony's father glided up towards us, slow and easy and smiling, and stopped right next to us, neat as a cat. I think that's the best day of my life. So far.

21
ABELA

Eventually the Tanzanian social services wrote to Judith Carrington to say they did not want to take Abela into their care. They had thousands of homeless children to care for, they told her, and though it was the way of Tanzanian families just to accept homeless relatives into their midst, there were still too many children to find homes for. They had located Abela's uncle, Thomas Mkumba, and his case was being investigated by the police. Anyway, he refused to be Abela's guardian, denying at first that he even knew her, even though they had papers where he was claiming to be her father in order to get a permit to return to England. They confirmed that they were investigating the charge that he had been involved in child trafficking. There was no way that he would be allowed back to England. They did not think he would be an appropriate person to bring up a little girl.

'Glory be!' Judith Carrington said out loud as she was reading the letter. 'How long did it take them to come to this conclusion?'

Another case conference was called, and Judith took the letter and read it aloud to Denis and her colleagues. 'In our opinion, it would be in Abela's best interest to stay in England, if a suitable home could be found for

202

her. We would be happy to support Miss Carrington's suggestion that Abela could be placed for adoption in England.' Judith put the letter down and looked round at the other social workers.

'She's a very, very brave child,' she said. 'But I think she's been through enough. She's been abandoned. I'd like to find an adoptive family for her as soon as possible.'

'Well,' said the team leader at last, rubbing his hair into spikes again. 'We can see that Abela is a special case. Has she been granted residence in this country?'

'Not yet,' Miss Carrington admitted. 'Nobody has applied for it.'

'Then that's the first step. If residence is not granted, she must be transferred to the care of the Tanzanian authority and that's the end of the matter. And if it is granted, then we'll take her case to the next adoption panel.'

He smiled at her. 'Any more clients to discuss?'

'They're not *clients*,' she said, as she did at every meeting. 'They're *children*. And I have forty on my books.' Forty young lives, and they were all in her care, all special cases. 'All needing hope.'

22
ROSA

It was a gorgeous summer that year, a summer of trips into Derbyshire, picnics at Padley Gorge and camping out at Edale, swimming in the open-air pool at Hathersage, cycling round Ladybower. Nana and Grandpa usually came with us, and, sometimes, Anthony and his father. He says we're an important part of Anthony's little life and he wants us to keep in touch with him. But I've seen the way he looks at Mum, and I've seen the way Mum looks at him. Nana sees it too, and no one says anything to anybody. Funny, isn't it? It's like a little candle just flickering in a still room. Don't breathe, or it might go out. Sometimes I daydream about us all living in the same house, but I don't mention it to a soul.

So when Mum said to me one day, 'Rosa, come over here a minute, I've got something very special to ask you,' I thought, this is it. The candle gleamed brightly for a moment and I hitched up a grin all over my face. But it wasn't that.

'How would you feel if we contacted Molly again?' she asked me. 'I'm ready to try again.'

23
ABELA

Abela knew nothing about all these meetings and case conferences, letters and phone calls that were going on. She had been appointed a solicitor and a guardian to look after her interests, and many people talked and argued and sighed over her case history. All she knew was that Mrs Oladipo talked to her more and was kinder to her. Mr Oladipo listened to her read every night after school, and chuckled deep in his belly when she got things wrong, and clapped his long flapping fingers together when she got them right. Cathy and Lola ignored her mostly, but they never teased her or bullied her. Lola was soon to be leaving the Oladipos, and she and Cathy were as close as sisters now, dreading the parting.

During the school summer holidays Jasmine phoned Abela to invite her to tea. Immediately, Abela ran upstairs and changed out of the yellow and green clothes that Carmel liked her to wear, into her kanga. She came downstairs with Mrs Long's cardigan draped over her arm. For the first time since she had left the hospital, she was smiling.

'I'm sorry, but you can't go,' Carmel told her.

Abela stared at her, her mouth open, her smile half-fading.

'No good looking at me like that,' Carmel said. 'You're in my care, Abela. I can't just let you go into any strange houses.'

'Please,' whispered Abela. She was beginning to tremble with a strange passion that she couldn't understand.

'No,' Carmel said. 'You can't. I'm your mum while you're with me. I'm saying no.'

It was then that Abela did something that she had never done before, that she did not even know how to do. She screamed, and she went on screaming, so loud and long that the sound seemed to come out of the walls of the house, down the stairs, through the windows, every brick and stone and pane of glass screamed with her. She threw herself on the ground and beat the rug with her fists, and when Mr Oladipo tried to lift her up she kicked out at him, twisting and turning violently, screaming, bellowing, yelling, raging with all the power and strength that her body possessed. There was no holding her down or quietening her, there was no comforting, there was only her pent-up rage, billowing and gathering and finally bursting out of her.

Carmel told me a few days later that Miss Carrington had been to see Jasmine's mother and father and said I could go and have tea there.

I think she wanted me to smile, but I didn't.

'Actually, Jasmine's mum asked if you could stay overnight.'

My insides bumped, but I still didn't smile.

'You can if you want. It's all right with me.'

Jasmine came with her father in their big black car to collect me. This time I knew my smile was coming but I didn't give it to Carmel or The Dad, I saved it for Jasmine. We sat in the back of the car and held hands and I let my smile out then. In the house I couldn't stop giggling, and neither could Jasmine. There were so many children that nobody noticed us giggling. We went up to bed straight after tea and tried each other's clothes on and giggled, and Jasmine brought her mother's beads in and we put them on, in our hair and round our necks and our wrists and our ankles, and we danced and shimmered and watched ourselves in the glass and giggled. We talked and whispered and laughed long after the other children and Jasmine's parents had gone to bed.

'I wish I could live here,' I said.

'I wish you could,' whispered Jasmine. 'You'd be my sister then.'

'My sister died,' I whispered back, after ever such a long time. 'Her name was Nyota. It means star.'

We lay with our arms round each other, too tired to talk, listening to the first songs of birds in the trees outside. I floated to sleep, and Jasmine shook me and said, 'I'll ask Mummy in the morning. She'll say yes.'

We went down to breakfast holding hands. The baby and the youngest boy were screaming. Jasmine's father was rushing to get ready for work, his tie flapping round his neck. The older brother was banging on the bathroom door, the older sister was shrieking to be allowed to shower in peace for once in her life. I sat at the table and smiled at everyone, and Jasmine said,

'Abela's coming to live here.'

'She's what?' said her mother, ladling mashed banana into the toddler's mouth, and a milky porridge into the baby's. She scooped the dribbles off their chins with the back of her finger.

'She can't stay at Mrs Oladipo's for ever, so she's going to live here.'

The little brother fell off his chair and screamed. The baby screamed too, squelching more gurgles of porridge down his chin. I stopped smiling.

'She can, can't she, Mum?'

'She can what?'

'Live here. Please, Mum. In my bedroom.'

'Jasmine, don't be ridiculous,' her father said.

'Nobody in her right mind would want to live here,' said her sister, who had come down at last from the bathroom with a towel wrapped round her dripping hair.

'Help yourself to some toast,' Jasmine's mother called over her shoulder. She hoicked up toddler and baby, one under each arm, to be washed and changed.

'Can she?' Jasmine appealed for the last time to anyone who might listen.

'No.'

'Never mind.' Jasmine juggled hot toast in each hand and ran across the kitchen to where I was sitting. 'You're still my sister.'

And when I went back to Carmel's house I told her, 'Jasmine's my sister.'

She laughed down at me, her big wet laugh.

'All my girls want sisters if they don't have them,' she said. 'And if they do have them, they wish they hadn't!'

'I'm going to live at her house when I leave here,' I said. I looked at Carmel sideways. I wondered if I was going to scream again, like that other time when all the house screamed back at me. I wondered what she would do if I did, whether she would hate me or hit me or send me away. I lifted up my fists ready to beat her and she bent down to me and said,

'One day soon, Miss Carrington's going to find you a lovely family to live with. But till then, I'm your mum, Abela, and this is your family. I'm taking care of you, as if you were one of my own.'

Lola was moving soon to live with a cousin and his wife who ran a hotel in the Lake District. They had given her a job there, helping in the kitchens, and she would have a room of her own under the eaves. She talked about it day and night when she came back from her first visit there. She said the house was like a mansion, with television and toilet and washbasin in every single room, shiny floors that made your shoes click when you walked on them, and views across a lake that was almost as big as the sea. Cathy was beside herself with envy and despair.

On the day Lola was due to leave they had a party for her. Carmel made a sponge cake and showed Abela how to smear the chocolate icing over it with the back of a knife.

'Abela helped to make this,' Carmel announced at teatime.

Lola slid something across the table to Abela, wrapped up in kitchen paper. It was the key-ring that Susie had given her. Later, Lola stood in the sunshine garden in a new dress and smiled for Mr Oladipo's camera. Soon her picture would be on the wall with all the other children who had stayed in the house. When she was leaving, she and Cathy clung to each other, sobbing.

'I hate it,' Cathy said. 'It's always the same. I just get used to someone, and they go back home, or they get adopted, or they go to another foster home, or I have to move. I hate it! I hate it!'

Mrs Oladipo spent a lot of time with her that night, while Abela and Mr Oladipo washed up the dishes in silence. And it was different without Lola; loud, shouting, tempestuous Lola. To her dismay, Abela was moved back into the big room with Cathy.

'I'm sorry, but I've got a boy coming next,' Mrs Oladipo said. 'He'll need that little yellow room you've got. And anyway, Cathy won't be here for much longer. She's promised me she's going to study hard now, to go into nursing. She'll be no bother.'

Abela shrank into herself again. She had loved the yellow room. The big room was echoey and the curtains flapped noisily at night, Cathy talked in her sleep and sulked when she was awake. And Abela was afraid, realising now that it was true; nobody stayed with the Oladipos for very long. What was going to happen to her? She had no idea. Miss Carrington hadn't been to see her for a month; Jasmine was on holiday in Pakistan. The days stretched on endlessly through the summer. Mr Oladipo took her to the library every week and she came home with seven books, one for every day, and read till she was wide-eyed with the wonder of imaginary worlds and people. She thought that she might be ten now. She had no idea when her birthday was, but she had been nine for so long that it must be due or passed. But she told no one. It didn't seem to be important.

Towards the end of the summer holidays, she heard Miss Carrington's voice in the garden and ran outside to meet her. Last time Miss Carrington had seen her, Abela had been shy and withdrawn, saying little, watching every movement with huge, frightened eyes, but never looking anyone in the face. Now she ran to Miss Carrington and held her hand, pulling her into the kitchen to show her the latest book she was reading, telling her the story of what had happened so far.

'Wait, hold on, poor Miss Carrington doesn't have to hear every word!' Mrs Oladipo laughed.

'You've done well,' the social worker told Mrs Oladipo. 'She's a different child now.'

'She doesn't have nightmares no more,' Mrs Oladipo said. 'And her sheets are always dry, aren't they, Abela. And' – she pinched Abela's tummy – 'she eats like a horse!'

Abela giggled and squirmed away from her.

'Well, I've come with good news for you both,' Miss Carrington said. 'First, Abela is now a resident of England. That means you can stay in this country for as long as you want, Abela.'

Abela frowned. 'I still go to Tanzania when I'm a doctor?'

'Of course you can! And I'm sure you will. But that's a long time away, Abela. Meanwhile we have to find somewhere for you to live.'

Abela looked anxiously at Mrs Oladipo. This was the news she had been dreading. 'But I live here.'

'Yes, you do, but Mr and Mrs Oladipo are foster parents. You know what that means? It means they just look after you for a bit while we find a family who will be yours for all your life.'

'I want to stay here.'

'Ooh, I'll be an old lady soon,' Mrs Oladipo said. 'You need a proper mum and dad with a bit more energy than me and The Dad have got.'

'I promise you won't leave here till I've found exactly the right family for you, one we both like.' Judith smiled at Abela. 'All children should have a family to look out for them and look after them when they're growing up. I want you to trust me. I want you to be happy.'

Abela nodded, biting her lip, feeling the burn of tears behind her eyes. But she did trust her. She was the one who had helped her mother, long ago and far away in Africa.

'You'll meet them and get to know them first. You'll see photos of them, and they'll see photos of you, even before you meet them. And if you don't like them, you don't go there.'

Abela fiddled with the zip of her green jacket. Carmel hummed noisily at the sink. She had been through this so many times, easing her children into being strong enough to be taken away from her. So strange, so painful, every time.

'I've got something here for you,' Miss Carrington said. She brought a red hardback notebook out of her bag. 'I'm going to help you to write this. It will be your life story book.'

'My life story?' Abela was mystified.

'Everything you can remember about your life can go in this. And you'll keep it for ever. Shall we start now?'

Abela nodded at her solemnly, and Mrs Oladipo stood up. 'I've got beds to make,' she said. 'We've got the new boy coming tomorrow. Sammy, he's called. Nice name. I'll leave you two to get on with it.'

Miss Carrington opened the book. 'Shall I write it, or you, Abela? This is going to have everything you want to say in it. You can draw pictures in it, and put photographs in, and write any memories you want to write. You don't have to start at the beginning. Start anywhere you like. Write anything you like.'

Abela took the book and opened it carefully. She stroked the cool, smooth pages. 'Now?' she asked.

Miss Carrington nodded. 'Yes, let's start now. I've

brought you a special pencil.' She gave her a pencil that glittered when she turned it, and had a rubber at the end.

For a long time they sat in silence.

'It's hard for you to remember when you were a baby,' Miss Carrington said. 'Shall we start with a best memory? Something about your mama, something you and Mama loved doing together.'

Abela's eyes went misty with concentration. 'We have a game,' she said at last.

'Good. Tell me about your game.'

And so, very slowly, Abela began to write. Sometimes she asked Miss Carrington how to say something, or how to spell it, and every now and again she would stop and read it out loud, and Miss Carrington would help her to put down the next bit. This was how her Life Story began, though it was not the beginning of her life. Maybe she was about four years old when this first happened.

We have a game, Mama and I, when we pound maize. When the corncobs have been drying in the sun for long enough, we shake off all the little yellow buds into a heap, and we pour them into a basket. They go tchick, tchick, as they trickle down. Then we grind the buds into flour. We pound it with the end of a long stick from a tree, which is just as tall as Mama. It takes so long that our legs ache and ache with standing and our arms are heavy with holding the branch and stamping it down again and again. We must do it for hours, every day when the corn is ripe, to make enough for our food, to make enough to sell. The sky is greasy and sweaty. Flies buzz round my face and walk on my skin, and because my hands are busy I can't brush them away. They crawl in my hair and I can't do anything about them. My head throbs and I'm thirsty and tired.

This is when the game starts. Just when I think I can't do any more, Mama shouts, 'One, Abela!' She raises her branch and then she lets go of it and she claps her hands before she catches it again.

After a bit, Miss Carrington stood up and crept out, and Abela didn't even notice, because she was lost in her memories.

Now that the panel had agreed that Abela should be placed for adoption, Miss Carrington wanted it to happen as soon as possible. She looked through the lists of potential adopters in her area and found no one suitable, no one who wanted a child of Abela's age. Tanzanian girl, age nine. Nobody quite fitted the bill. She looked then through letters that had been sent from other authorities while she had been away. So many childless couples. So many people in need of someone to make their lives complete. So many desperate, generous, deserving families. But no one looking for a nine-year-old Tanzanian girl. She sent Abela's details to the magazine that went out to all families who were looking for a child to adopt. She flicked through the latest edition, at page after page of children's faces smiling confidently out of their troubled pasts. So many children needing love.

It was late, and she was tired, but memories of Abela kept flitting through her mind. Abela propping up her mother to help her out of the bus. Abela lying in hospital, closed up against the world that had taken her mother, father, baby sister and grandmother away from her. Abela laughing and skipping out to meet her that morning. Abela lost in a daydream of memories.

She had three more letters to read in her file, and then she would go home. One had been sent when she was still abroad and had never been brought to her notice. It came from a colleague in Sheffield, Molly West. They had trained together in Liverpool, and still kept in touch from time to time, usually about work matters. She skimmed through the letter, then read it again.

'We have a client looking for a Tanzanian child, preferably a girl, preferably junior school age.'

Judith looked at her watch and picked up the phone. Molly West might have finished work for the day, but she might just be working late, like Judith. It was worth a try. Her hand rested on the receiver, and then withdrew. Was it fair to nail down a family for Abela yet? The little girl was very plucky, she was coping well, but she still had a lot of grief to work through. What if the placement turned out to be unsuitable? It was unthinkable to risk moving her somewhere that wasn't right for her. And Sheffield was so far away, it would be hard for her to keep up regular visits while the pre-adoption placement was happening.

And yet it was so hard to find a family willing to adopt a girl of Abela's age, particularly if she was from another culture. She looked at Molly's letter again. It was three months since she had sent it. This family was probably fixed up by now. Anything at all could have happened in the meantime. Yet could she risk missing a chance like this? She tidied up her desk for the night and left the letter from Molly on the top. She would sleep on it, she decided.

24
ROSA

On a wet day, soon after the new school term started, I came home to find Molly having tea with Mum. I was so pleased to see her again that I went up and hugged her, just like I do with all my favourites of Mum's friends. I was about to sneak a look down to find out what shoes she was wearing when I saw that she was holding a photograph. A little girl of nine or ten looked solemnly up at me. She had her face cocked slightly to one side, like a bird, and her fingers made a little tent under her chin.

'Who's that?' I asked casually. My heart was doing a pumpity-pump excited dance. *Little sister, little sister,* my blood sang in my ears. *Little sister, little sister.*

'Her name is Abela Mbisi,' said Molly. 'I've just been telling your mum about her. I've been sent her details from the adoption services in London. She's been through a terrible time, this little girl.'

She passed the photograph across to Mum.

'It's so important to find the right home for her, as soon as possible. She needs so much love and a secure home. And of course, the first people I thought about were you two. She fits your initial application absolutely, and no one else in my area has made a similar request. I just wondered if you would like to come and meet her.'

I hardly dared look at Mum.

'There is one problem, that I have to tell you now,' Molly went on. 'Her parents both died of Aids.'

I gasped. What about Abela? Could she have it too?

As if she was reading my thoughts, Molly said, 'I don't know, at the moment, whether the little girl has been tested for HIV.'

The silence went on for ever. I knew a lot about Aids from television programmes and school. I knew that it was a terrible problem, particularly in parts of Africa.

'And if she has it?' Mum asked.

'Aids is not always the killer disease it used to be. These days, especially in the West, treatment is very effective.'

If Mum were to adopt Abela and she got ill, it would be really, really hard for her. But Mum would be thinking something else as well, I knew. To give a chance of happiness to someone in this situation is a rare gift. I'd heard Mum say that so often. Putting money in a charity box is easy, she says. Taking a bundle of cast-off clothes to Oxfam costs you nothing at all. But this was something that would affect our lives, for ever. And I willed her to say yes. *Your mother has so much love to give*, Nana had said. Well, so have I. We can do it. We can do it together, Mum. I went and stood behind her, touching her just lightly on the shoulder. It's what she does to me sometimes, when I need a bit of support.

'Yes,' said Mum at last. 'I'll come and meet her.'

25
ABELA

Abela spent hours writing in her book, slowly and painfully, struggling to write in English as much as in Swahili, struggling to bring her memories to the surface. When she wasn't writing there was a voice in her head, framing the words that she would later struggle to put on the page. She felt she was talking aloud to someone when she was writing, someone who understood her and wanted to be her friend.

'Want any help?' Carmel asked her one day. She worried that Abela was spending so much time up in her room on her own.

'I write my life story,' Abela said shyly.

'Your life story! All nine years of it!' Carmel smiled. 'Good job no one asked me to write mine. Sixty years, I've got to tell about, and every one like a rainbow! You want some help?'

'I can't remember everything,' Abela admitted.

'Show me some of the things you brought with you. Show me your pretty kangas! I bet they've got stories to tell!'

Abela ran upstairs and brought her two kangas down and spread them on the table. 'They've got words printed on them,' Carmel said. 'Can you tell me what they mean?'

'This one mean "You will remember me",' said Abela shyly. 'And this one mean "Be my friend".'

'Oh, I'd like one that says, "Come and do my housework!"' Carmel laughed. 'Where can I buy it? Marks & Spencer's?'

Abela giggled. 'We have a big market, where they sell them. They sell everything there. All kinds of fruit, chickens, beans ... And cloths like this. Some is bright cotton like this. And some is not heavy, like the Asian ladies wear.'

'Oh, don't I love markets! Tell me what it was like, Abela. Did your mum sell things there?'

Abela nodded. She closed her eyes and swayed on the balls of her feet as she described the shady, covered stalls of the main market and the open square where she and her mother and the poorest women used to sit. She told about the little mounds of oranges and bananas, red beans, chilli peppers, the live chickens, the thieving dogs and cats. She flicked her eyes open dramatically and told Carmel about the mad mzee with her curved, deadly panga, chasing the children and the teacher round the stalls. Carmel shrieked with laughter.

'No wonder you can run like a gazelle. Poor old woman though. Some old people just lose their minds, you know. Sometimes life gets so bad for them, they don't know what they're doing any more. I used to go to the library every week for an old lady on the corner who couldn't even walk that far. And one day, I brought her a book she'd already had, and do you know what she said? She was going to boil my head in the stewpot! I never ran so fast in my life!'

'I write now,' Abela said. Carmel would talk all day if she let her.

'OK, my love. I'll leave you to it.'

Another time, on one of the social worker's visits, Abela showed Judith Carrington the sloppy sandals and told her about Bibi's friend who had given them to her.

'What's she like, Abela? Can you see her in your mind?'

Abela frowned, trying to catch the slippery picture before it disappeared. 'She fat. She has a bit of tooth missing, here. She cooks good *mayai*.'

'*Mayai*, that's egg, isn't it? I remember that.'

Abela chuckled. '*Mayai yanavyovurugwa*.'

'My goodness! You've got me there! What's that?'

Abela flicked her fingers together rapidly.

'Oh, I know! Scrambled egg!' They both laughed. 'You'd better put that in your book, Abela. Can't have you forgetting a word like that!'

After she had written it down, giggling again as they tried to imagine how to spell it, Abela let the pencil roll away from her. She sat with her head bowed, clenching and unclenching her fingers.

'Is there something else about her?' Judith asked.

Slowly, half-whispering, Abela told her then how Bibi and the same friend had held her down under the flame tree while the medicine woman cut her. She

222

described how she had been looking up at the blinding yellow sun but had been too frightened to close her eyes in case Bibi thought she was dead. She told how she had heard the green monkeys screaming and had wanted to put her own screams among them, but that Bibi's hand was pressed over her mouth so she couldn't make any scream at all. She told her about the angel wings beating about her head until everything was dark and peaceful. And afterwards, how Bibi and her friend had taken it in turns to wash her with water scented with healing herbs, and had sung to her in their deep warm red voices.

The social worker did not write this down. When Abela had finished talking she closed up the book and said, 'You've remembered that very well, Abela. I wonder if you're angry with Bibi for letting it happen?'

Abela was silent, clenching her fists until her knuckles were white. She felt her screams rising inside her, then spreading out, dissolving. She nursed her top lip inside her bottom teeth. Then she nodded. Her tears scalded her eyes.

'Well, you know, I don't think Bibi wanted to hurt you. She did it because she thought it was the right thing to do to girls; the same thing happened to her, and to her mother, and her mother before that. But many people realise now that it is not a good thing to do, and they're able to stop doing it.'

'When I'm a doctor, I'll tell them,' Abela said.

'That's right,' Judith smiled. 'When you're a doctor, they'll listen to you. You'll be a wise woman!'

'I am wise,' Abela nodded thoughtfully. 'I think I am ten years old now.'

'Really? When was your birthday?'

Abela shrugged. 'I don't know. But I think I am ten now.'

'Well, that's quite old. D'you think you're too old to play Snakes and Ladders with Cathy?'

'I love Snakes and Ladders!' Abela giggled. 'I'll even play it when I'm as old as Bibi!'

Judith persuaded Cathy to come down and have a break from her homework. She stumped downstairs, moaning that her brain was hurting, and Carmel produced her battered compendium of games from the cupboard by the fireplace.

'Do I have to?' Cathy moaned, but she caught Carmel's look, raised her eyebrows in despair and slid down onto the chair next to Abela. In minutes Abela's mood had changed; she was bright and quick with laughter, full of the fun of the game. Judith tidied the objects that Abela had brought downstairs to write about, and flicked through the animal book that Abela and Susie had made.

'What a lovely book – but who scribbled in it?' she asked. 'Was it you, Abela?'

'It was me,' said Cathy, blushing to the roots of her hair. 'Me and Lola.'

'Then you can just rub them out,' Carmel said. 'What a mess!'

She took the book and opened it at the last page. 'What's this?' she asked.

Judith studied the certificate for a moment, and then smiled and nodded. 'It's just about the most important piece of paper Abela could have,' she said. 'It's going to save us all a great deal of anguish. Fancy it being here all the time! I'll look after it for her now.' She prised up the Sellotape that Susie had used, and put the HIV/Aids certificate carefully in her folder. Then she gave Cathy the book.

'Do your best with it,' she told her. 'It's precious.'

She paused in the doorway for a moment, watching the girls with their heads bent together over the board game, then went out to her car. Carmel followed her out.

'She's such a plucky kid!' Carmel said. 'I don't think I've ever come across a child who's been through so much, and I probably don't know the half of it.'

'The main thing is, she's coming through it. Every time I see her she looks better. You're doing very well with her, Carmel.'

'I love that child,' Carmel admitted. 'Don't say that about all of them, do I? Glad to see the back of some of them, however hard I've tried.' She shook her head, laughing, wiping her eyes with the back of her hand. 'But this little one...We got off to a bad start, and it was my fault. Never looked after a little girl before. But we're OK now. The Dad thinks as much of her as I do. Let's hope nothing else goes wrong in her life. Will someone adopt her?'

'At her age, who can tell? But I have made a contact, I think.' Judith looked down at her notes. 'Six more children to visit today, and they've all got their own problems. I'd better get a move on!'

After that, Carmel helped Abela to write in her book every day, while Cathy was doing her homework. It was the quiet time, she said. Time to sit down and rest her feet.

'My toes are like big balloons, just look at them! Go on now, tell me the story of your long life!' she would say to Abela. 'What've you got to show me today?'

Abela would run upstairs and sort through her things in the bedside cupboard; sometimes she would choose Mrs Long's cardigan or the beaded-mirror key-ring, or the book of animals that she and Susie had drawn. It was some time before she chose the Coca-Cola car.

'This my best thing,' she told Carmel. 'My baba make me this car.'

'Ah, now you tell me, I can see it's meant to be a car!' Carmel tried to make the squashed wheels turn on the tabletop. 'But I must say it just looks like a battered old tin can. Shall we write about this today?'

'Me write!' said Abela, putting on a baby voice. She loved this time, this special time of day that was just for her.

'Say it properly.'

'I'll write it.' Abela giggled.

'That's better. Write about your daddy.'

Abela's eyes clouded. It was so long now since her father died. His face slid in and out of her memory, like a fish drifting in and out of shadowed water. She couldn't hold it there. She couldn't see him.

226

'Was he like The Dad?' Carmel prompted. 'Like a great quiet grizzly grumpy old bear?' She hooted with laughter.

Abela shook her head. 'Baba is a big, strong man,' she wrote. 'He is my father. He has walked many miles and he has climbed many hills. But he has not been to England. He has not been to any town. He has not been on a bus.' She stared into space, trying to see again the man who was her father, trying to smell his warm skin and feel the soft touch of his hands on her face, trying to hear the brown rumble of his singing in church. 'He has a black cow called Yetu. And one day he sold the cow to a man in another village, and we were all sad. We said goodbye to Yetu and my father walked her away. I ran after them and kept slapping Yetu's bottom to say goodbye, till Baba turned round and told me to go to school. At school I drew a picture of Yetu on my slate.'

Carmel read over her shoulder and laughed. 'Tell me something about your father, not about your cow!'

'He could sing like Yetu,' Abela told her, giggling. She deepened her voice and mooed like a cow. 'Lovely big voice. And he made me this car.'

She held the car in both her hands, remembering how Baba had shaped the wheels by cutting pieces of tin and flattening them with a stick, curling the strips round a little rod. She could hear his slow, thoughtful breathing as he worked, rumbling his Yetu song to make her laugh; she could see again how he had squatted on his haunches to make the car roll on the ground for the very first time.

But now the Coca-Cola tin body was squashed and scratched, the wheels were flattened and useless. She put the car down and took up her pencil again.

'In the night we heard a big loud noise outside, and we ran to see what it was,' she wrote. Her tongue flickered on her lips as she concentrated. 'It was Yetu! She had walked all the way home from the other village. Now my baba says she can stay with us, and we give the money back to the man who borted her, and we put beans in the ground instead of eating them, so they will grow and we can sell them.'

'And they grew right up to the sky! Fee fie fo fum!' laughed Carmel. 'B.o.u.g.h.t., honey. Hang on.'

She went outside to speak to her husband, who was easing caterpillars off his cabbages. After a bit he came into the kitchen carrying the toolbox from the shed. While Abela was writing he took up her car and began to prise the flattened wheels from the bodywork, coiling them round to make them roll again. Carmel sent Cathy to the local shop to buy a tin of Coke, then poured it out for them to share, grinning at them because fizzy drinks were usually forbidden. The girls hiccupped as it went down too fast. The Dad fixed the wheels onto the new Coke tin, testing it from time to time on the tabletop by rolling it carefully backwards and forwards. During all this time he never spoke a word, just whistled very slightly between his teeth like a sissing snake, but when he had finished he handed the car to Abela and said, 'This isn't as good as the way your daddy made it. I'm all thumbs these days.'

And at that moment Carmel snapped her camera and there was Abela, clutching her new car and smiling with joy.

The next time Miss Carrington visited, Abela was writing about the red cardigan and the yellow echoey schoolhouse in Tanzania. In her daydreams insects buzzed and hummed around her head, a laughing jackass shrieked in the trees outside, children chanted their tables as Mrs Long wrote them out on the board. 'Mrs Long has curly black hair,' Abela wrote. 'Mrs Long is so kind.'

'Would you like to write a letter to your teacher?' Judith asked her. 'I'm sure we can find a way of getting it to her. She'd love to know how you are, Abela.'

'Can I?' Abela's eyes were wide with surprise.

Carmel brought her a piece of writing paper and Abela stared at it for a long time, as if she expected words to appear on it by magic.

'Dear Mrs Long,' Carmel prompted her.

Abela licked her lips carefully and wrote, 'Dear Missus Long.' Then she looked up. 'What else will I write?' she whispered.

'Anything,' Judith said. 'What would you say to her if you met her in the street now?'

'Hello, Teacha. How are you?' Abela said shyly. She began to write, 'I am very well. I am very happy. I have a friend called Jasmine and a friend called Carmel and a friend called Cathy and The Dad who mend my car is

229

my friend and I have a friend called Judith and she is my' – she paused – 'soshal werker. I see her in Africa. Abela.'

Judith read the letter and smiled. 'Do you know, Abela, this will make Mrs Long very, very happy. I'll find out where to send it and I'll post it today. Now, I've got something important to tell you.'

'Uh oh! Cup of tea time!' Carmel sang. She went over to the sink and closed her eyes tight. This was the moment she longed for and dreaded with every child who came into her care.

'You know we've talked in the past about *one day*, when you'll move on to live with a new family, the family you'll stay with for the rest of your life?' Judith asked.

Abela nodded solemnly. She could see Carmel, standing by the sink with her back to her. It was as if a chasm was opening up between them, dark and deep and frightening. Miss Carrington's voice was coming to her from far away, from the other side of her world, the other side of her life.

'Well, we've found someone who might be just right. Tomorrow a lady is coming to see you. She's looking for a little girl just like you to adopt, and she'd like to meet you.'

Carmel turned round, smiling encouragement at her. 'That's lovely, honey. Someone who can give you a nice home for your life. You're ready for a nice family all of your own.'

'No promises on either side,' Judith told her. 'Just

meet her and see if you like her. I won't let you go anywhere if you're not happy with the idea. But I'd like you to meet her.'

'But I don't want.' Abela stared down at her letter to Mrs Long. She remembered her teacher's words, *Be happy, Abela*. She had wondered then if she could ever be happy again, and since then she had often wondered whether there was anyone in the world she could trust. But now she was beginning to be happy again, and she could trust Miss Carrington and Carmel. If they thought it was a good thing to meet this lady, then she must do it.

'I've brought a photograph of her.' Judith took a picture out of her bag, and Abela looked sideways at it, the smiling, friendly face, the floppy brown hair. She looked kind.

'Her name's Jen Warren. There isn't a daddy in the house,' Judith went on. 'Just this lady and her daughter. This is Rosa.'

'She is like me,' Abela whispered, surprised.

'Well, she is. A bit like you. Her daddy came from Tanzania too.'

Abela held the photograph in her hands. She turned it over, and then looked at it again, at the happy, friendly, smiling face of the girl who might become her big sister.

'All right,' she whispered. 'I try.'

But as soon as Miss Carrington had gone she burst into tears. Carmel stood with her arms round her, rocking her gently backwards and forwards, backwards and forwards.

'There, there', she said. 'You cry, honey, You cry. That's real good. That's real good.'

26
ROSA

And that was how my little sister came to live with us. It seems like ages ago now; it feels as if she has always lived here. But it was ages before it all happened. I couldn't believe how long it took, all those meetings, all those talks. Mum met her, and I met her, and she came for tea, and she came for a weekend, and she came skating with me and hated it and fell over and cried. She met Nana and Grandpa, and loved them. And at last she moved in with her little bag of belongings. I was so excited that day, so proud and nervous. I took her to meet some of my friends, the ones who had adopted Twitchy's kittens.

'This is my sister, Abela.'

I'm used to saying that now.

Abela started at our local primary school, the one I used to go to, after Christmas. Mum met her every day and walked through the park with her, holding her hand. She had three months' adoption leave, just as if she'd had a new baby.

Abela didn't call her anything at first, but then she started calling her Mummy. That was strange, but nice too, and right. I taught her how to make apricot slices. At first Mum talked to her a lot in Swahili, and I felt really out of it, and so they started to teach it to me. It's like a secret language now, that the three of us share when we're out together. Often Mum talks to us both about Africa, but she always talks about the good things, the friendly people and the proud, strong women that she knew when she was there, the beautiful places she has seen in the towns and in the countryside. We'll go there, one day, very soon. Mum's already saving up. She, Abela and I are going to Africa, to Tanzania, to Abela's country and to mine. It's our promise to each other, our holiday in Africa, and nothing, nothing is going to stop us doing it.

Her English is getting better all the time, but she likes me to do 'lessons' with her. I help her to write letters to Mrs Long and to Carmel. She's so funny, the way the tip of her tongue wriggles on her bottom lip when she's writing. She covers the letters with pictures of animals, birds, flowers, and kisses. Her friend Jasmine came to stay for a weekend, and they giggled and cried so much that I got fed up and moved into Anthony's room. It's still his room, he comes to stay occasionally. I haven't got anywhere of my own any more, just mine.

And then, Adoption Day came, in the Easter holidays. We all went to the County Court: Mum, Grandpa, Nana, me and Abela, and Judith Carrington and Molly and some other people who we didn't know. It wasn't a big exciting place like they have in TV courtroom dramas; it was just a sort of office. We all sat round the biggest, shiniest table I've ever seen, with the judge at one end.

She wasn't at all frightening; a gentle-looking woman with droopy eyelids and amazing fluffy hair, just dressed in ordinary clothes, which was a bit disappointing. My stomach was doing its butterfly quaking, and goodness knows how Mum and Abela were feeling, holding hands next to me. But everyone smiled, the papers were signed, and it was all over in two minutes.

Abela asked the judge where her wig was, and the judge sent the clerk to fetch it and then put it on Abela's head, and we took a photograph of her; one huge smile under a frosty grey wig. Grandpa called her the wise old bird after that.

So that's how she became my little sister. It still isn't easy, for me or for Mum or for her. I got jealous when Grandpa started to teach her piano, but as soon as she was adopted he bought her a guitar and paid for her to have lessons on that instead. She sings when she's playing, in a lovely, high, golden-yellow voice.

I love it when Mum and I go out together, skating or shopping, just us, and leave Abela with Nana. I love it when I go to Grandpa's on my own for my piano lesson. But I love it, too, when Abela and I do things together. She's so funny, she's got a giggle that's like a stream bubbling, and once she starts, I get it too. We drive Mum mad when we're giggling.

We squabble sometimes. I pull her hair and she scratches me. She wants to know my secrets. She hangs around listening when my friends come round, when I just want to be on my own with them and dance in our bedroom and have a good time and talk about the boys we're crazy about. It's a real drag, sometimes, having her around.

And I have a sense that deep down, she's wiser and cleverer than me, she knows things that I will never know and she has seen things that I will never see; she'll do things that I will never do. I look into the blackness of her eyes and I see wild creatures and unknown frightening places and unbearable sorrow. She has come through all those things; but they're part of her for ever, they have made her what she is. I think she will become a great person.

I wouldn't be without her. Not for anything in the world. I love her, really love her. And she loves us. She's my little sister, and we're her for ever family. She belongs.

ACKNOWLEDGEMENTS

A little girl called Halima made a great impression on me. This story is not about her, but it is because of meeting her that I wanted to write it.

I talked to many people while I was writing *Abela: The Girl Who Saw Lions*, and would like to thank in particular Julie Jarman, Dolores Long, Tricia Murray-Leslie, Helen Kendal and the Adoption Team in Sheffield, Maria Oldroyd from the Asylum Seekers Unit in Sheffield, Pat Reed and, of course, my husband Alan Brown for his enormous encouragement.